WELCOME TO THE GREY ZONE...

...And its nefarious and shadowy landscape that knows no international borders.

....Whose each and every individual has special expertise, but no permanent ties or allegiances to any nationalities, countries, or governments. If you want a landmark statue shattered in New York City, a bridge blown in London, a tower toppled in Paris—but don't want any evidence left around to tie you to the crimes—you'll find people in the GREY ZONE who'll sign on to accomplish any and all of that—for a price!

Freelance special agents Roger Lenic, Terrence Flag, and Howard Cahn are among those in the GREY ZONE who are about to be—or already have been—recently hired...to bury the *INCIDENT AT ABERLENE*!

INCIDENT AT ABERLENE

SPIES AND LIES, BOOK ONE

WILLIAM MALTESE

THE BORGO PRESS

MMXI

INCIDENT AT ABERLENE

DEDICATION

For John Betancourt, Publisher

and

Michael Burgess, Editor

Without whose double-vision there would be none of
these Wildside/Borgo double-novel books

Contents

CHAPTER ONE

CORT GRAMLIN'S BLOOD? Her blood? *Their* bloods?

Scarlet and crimson. Carmine and vermillion. Garnet and Ruby.

All over him. All over her. All over the room.

Splattered. Streaked. Smeared. Soaked.

He had done a very messy job of it! A damned messy job!

The blood stunk: rich, rotten. Its coagulation was turning his underpants stiff, like a coating of dried semen. Its gumminess was on his fingers, like glue.

He moved the fingers of his bloody right hand, feeling the bloody pain.

"Damn it! Damn it!" His right index finger was damaged. He had sprained it, or, maybe, even fractured it. Of all goddamned fingers, it had to be his trigger finger. More complications! He looked at the corpse on the floor, for not the first time. "Bitch!" he accused it-once-her.

The kill was sloppy, because he had really had no intentions of killing Pam Dyne. Killing her had been the last thing on his mind when he'd come to her apartment. Hell, he had loved the woman. At least, that's what he'd told himself, despite all of the bells gone off inside his brain, warning that love wasn't authorized in his business.

He had goddamned loved her, nevertheless! Loved a she-bitch who had manipulated him like a marionette on strings. Damn, what a clever, clever bitch, sucking him in deeper and deeper, conjuring emotions he'd successfully kept hidden for years; prying them out, one by one, along with the dangerous emotions of caring, wanting, needing, trusting. All she'd been heading him toward had been this final bloody moment that had turned against her.

She would have won, if he hadn't, for whatever the reason, come awake to see her with gun in hand.

His spontaneous laugh, now, was caused from nerves not from amusement, and it was quickly aborted when pain, from his damaged finger, shot through his hand and forearm. Would he ever know why he awoke? Would he ever know how his reflexes had automatically sent him on the defensive, even against the woman he loved?

There was certainly nothing to laugh about. None of it was funny. There, on the floor, dead, if not because of some fluke of fate, could have been him. There, in fact, *should* have been him. Even he had difficulty summoning any replay that explained how he'd apparently managed to survive unscathed except for one damaged finger. She'd had the gun. He'd had nothing except the vase he'd grabbed from the bedside table and shattered, sending its roses, red like the blood, onto the carpet. Eventually, he'd used the jagged edges to hack away her life. But, how had he gotten to her through the barrage of bullets popping out of the silencer to whistle around his ears?

Maybe he was hit and didn't know it. Pain was sometimes concealed beneath surges of adrenaline jetted throughout the nervous system in times of extreme excitation. He paused a moment, telling himself to be calm, telling his heart to be still in its frantic beating. He took systematic stock, summoning all of his expertise in concentration to survey, systematically, his body and its parts in an effort to determine which, if any, of the blood splattering him was his instead of hers.

He'd known a fellow agent once, Tom Slister. They'd done an assignment in Germany which had seen them exiting in a rain of gunfire.

"Are you okay, Tom?" Cort asked during their crouch in the

darkness of an alley.

"I'm fucking fine, man," Tom assured. "Fucking-A!"

He'd been hit five times, bleeding like a stuck pig, leaving the trail of blood that pinpointed them as surely as any arrow. It wasn't until the safe house, though, both thinking they'd made safety, the lights on, that they realized otherwise. The irony was how Tom, even then, didn't seem to comprehend he was dying. He looked at his blood as if it wasn't his, more likely just paint picked up when he'd inadvertently leaned against a newly redecorated fence or wall. To this day, Cort doubted the sonfoabitch had any real clue, even as Tom gave up the ghost.

If Cort was now wounded, he had to find and identify the wound before he bled to death as unknowingly as Tom Slister.

He stood before the full-length mirror that veneered the sliding doors of the walk-in closet. It was the same mirror that had reflected Pam and his lovemaking. It was the same that reflected her corpse, now. Quickly, he examined his tightly muscled chest and rippled abdominals. No bullet holes. He turned his back to the mirror, glancing over his shoulder. No wounds to be seen there, either. He leaned forward, patting down each leg. He dropped his bloody underpants. Jesus, his prick was shriveled so far into his pubic hair that it was almost impossible to see. He thought for a moment one of the shots had blasted it away.

Finally, relieved at finding little wrong except for his blood-splattered condition and his bad finger, he found his clothes and dressed. All of the time, he kept trying to figure out how he was going to clean up the mess. It wasn't just this mess that was worrying him, either. He had an assignment which he was expected to fulfill, now impossible with his finger the way it was. There was no way he could pull a trigger. Already, the injury had turned most of his right hand numb. He couldn't hold a gun, let alone shoot one.

Problems! Jesus, problems!

He told himself to keep his cool, nothing ever gained, a hell of a lot lost, by panicking in a crisis. He walked over to the array of liquor bottles on a nearby table. He poured himself a full tumbler of Scotch. For the moment, he wasn't concerned with the bloody fingerprints he left on the bottle and glass. Hell, his fingerprints were all over this apartment; they had been even before this catastrophe. Everything, but everything, had to be wiped down to erase his presence from the room.

He collapsed into a chair, feeling sick to his stomach, telling himself this wasn't the time or the place to fall to pieces. There would be time enough for that later. Between then and now, he had to think things out. He had to find a solution to this mess and to his other pressing commitment. So, calmly, coolly, what did he do now?

He finished his Scotch, got up from the chair, and went to the telephone. He had a few markers he could call in, a few favors done that warranted repayment. He would cash in, now. He had no other choice. There was no conceivable way he cleaned up this mess by himself. It called for professionals, and there were several such teams from which to choose: FBI, CIA, Special Ops…. He dialed. The voice that answered did nothing but repeat the number dialed.

"Davenport Cleanup?" Cort asked, wondering if the CIA had changed field numbers. It had been some time since he'd found it necessary to utilize this exchange. Not since the Delanson caper which had put the regional CIA director in Cort's debt.

"They haven't been here for quite some time," the woman's voice said. He tried to picture what she looked like, unable to summon up any female image but that of the dead one on the floor.

Cort began to sweat, the full impact of what had happened suddenly dawning. The sheer precariousness of his situation ate his guts. He was in bad shape here, whether wounded or not. He had put himself into a compromising position that could endanger far bigger things than what had gone down in this room.

"Their number has been changed to…," she said, giving Cort's memory what it needed for him to make the second call.

He dialed.

Another voice. Another repeat of the number dialed.

"Davenport Cleanup?" Cort asked, hearing the nervousness in his voice.

"One moment, please," the voice, male this time, said.

His call was transferred to another line. He heard all of the accompanying electronic clicks.

"Davenport Cleanup!" another voice proclaimed, so surprisingly loudly and clearly that it might have been from in the same room with Cort. Cort glanced nervously around. "Davenport Cleanup," the voice repeated.

"I have a job for you," Cort said. "Mr. Sanders has authorized the call." Cal Sanders was the Regional CIA Director who would have had a bullet hole in his chest if Cort hadn't acted fast in getting the overweight man out of the line of fire on a job a few months back. "It's a compete sweep," Cort continued, indicating nothing should be left remaining in evidence. A clean sweep was only required for the messiest kills. It was taken for granted there would be at least one body that needed disposing.

"One or more rooms?" the voice asked, showing very little, if any, emotion. The man was a professional and wasn't really asking about rooms at all. A clean sweep called for a complete gutting of the premises, no matter how many rooms.

"Just one," Cort provided the body-count, wishing the liquor was closer. He needed another drink. "The room in question rather soiled," he said, even though that likely went without saying.

"You say, Mr. Sanders told you to call?"

"Yes," Cort said, suddenly fearful that Sanders might have been transferred elsewhere. It had been months since Cort's heroics saved the bastard's fat ass. It was just Cort's declining luck to have Sanders not around when he needed him to authorize this salvage. "Countersign Chlidon, Dylon," he said, Dylon Chlidon was Cort's cover on the CIA assignment in question.

"May we have the job address, Mr. Chlidon?" the man asked. With relief, Cort told him. Everything else would supposedly be hashed out later. To have done so now would waste valuable time and contribute to complications that could occur in leaving any body and body of evidence too long lying around.

When he replaced the phone on its receiver, he was trembling. A very bad sign. He was a professional, goddamn it! All of this should run off his back like water shed by a duck. It should make no difference that he had loved Pam, or that she had tried to kill him, or that he *had* killed her. The trouble was, of course, it did matter? The years of doing what he did were beginning to show by way of wear and tear on his nerves. He had reached that point he had always dreaded reaching, at which he had always promised himself he would recognize how the balance of his continued survival had likely tipped against him in warning that it was time for him to get out of the business. Well, if he did get out, it wouldn't be a smooth exit if he didn't find some way of fulfilling a final commitment suddenly made impossible by his injured finger. The people who had contracted him, and paid him, wouldn't understand anything but his trying to back out on a deal which had been signed and sealed before the unscheduled events of this evening.

He had another drink but only one, knowing that the cleanup crew wouldn't waste any time getting to the scene. In his kind of business, time was of the essence. It was *de rigueur* to vacate, and quickly, after a call; not doing so could lead the cleanup crew to suppose you were the enemy rather than a friend. The later could be very detrimental to any slow-poke's health.

He went down the stairs and out through the garage. He wore gloves to keep his bloody hand from leaving any kind of trial that might link him to events after the cleanup crew did its job. Probably, he should have washed up in Pam's bathroom, even taken a shower, but he'd wanted out of there, once he'd decided how it would happen; he could shower at his own apartment. He passed several people while he made his way to his car, but no one—thank God!—seemed to pay him any mind.

It was a half-hour drive across town to his apartment. He had chosen his residence carefully, making sure no doorman could pinpoint his arrivals and departures. He could thank God for that precaution, now, especially when he realized, with a start, that the left side of his head had blood-clotted hair.

He was cold when he reached his room, shutting the door behind him and locking it. No matter that it was a balmy night, his room hardly chilly.

In the bathroom mirror, his face was glossed with sweat, despite his continuing shivers. This mirror verified the dark blood in his dark hair was hardly noticeable. Quickly, he shed his gloves and clothes to reveal more incriminating evidence: his undershorts painted with blood.

He stepped out of his shorts, leaving them and the rest of his clothes on the floor as he adjusted the spray in the shower stall. The water was really too hot when he stepped into it, but he left it that way. He derived masochistic satisfaction in the pain from the burning water, assured that its scalding intensity would somehow achieve a cleansing that wouldn't be accomplished at a more temperate Fahrenheit.

Red streamers of water-dissolved blood trailed his face, chest, belly, thighs, eventually to vortex down the drain. He soap-lathered his body, and, then, lathered it again, telling himself that this blood was no different from any of the other blood with which he'd been splattered during his long career as an free-lance agent within the murky Grey Zone. Except this was the blood of the woman he had loved, the blood of the woman he had been willing to give up his old life in order to marry.

She had tried to kill him. Why? He still didn't know. Things had happened too quickly for him to ask. His reaction to seeing her with that gun had been reflexive, done without any conscious thought. Automatic impulses, primitive needs for survival, prompted him, leaving Pam dead, leaving him alive with unanswered questions.

Not that there wasn't a whole gamut of possibilities as to why she'd done it. People in Cort's line of business made all kinds of enemies who held grudges for long periods. Any of his enemies could have hired Pam to kill him. Hell, possibilities were endless. Even people for whom he had worked and carried out successful assignments might be after his head, figuring he knew too much, in retrospect, about their businesses.

Of course, his finding out who was behind his attempted murder wasn't his only pressing problem. He had that termination scheduled which couldn't be put off, and he was no longer the finely tuned executioner required for the job. His index finger was swollen to twice its normal size, the skin beginning to discolor. Whether broken or not, it incapacitated him in the one area of his expertise that he couldn't presently afford. He was locked into a job assignment, delivery promised and paid for in full; even if he was in no position to perform and deliver.

"Pam, you goddamned bitch!" he said aloud; he would have killed her if he hadn't done so already. Briefly, he wondered whether the cleanup crew had her in a body bag, by now, lugging her, as discreetly as possible, down the backstairs. Goddamn, that woman had thoroughly screwed his life royally.

He soaped down yet again, waiting for the revelation that would deliver him. Such insights had occurred in the shower, before, and he awaited one now. There had to be a viable way out!

Out of the shower, he sidestepped his bloody clothes, and dried while seeing himself reflected, this time, within a section of bathroom mirror surprisingly not misted with steam.

Considering everything, he looked damned good for his thirty-nine years. It hadn't been false egotism which had allowed him to accept Pam's compliments regarding his good looks and well-muscled body. What it had been was merely self-acceptance that he *was* handsome, and he *did* have the good looks and athletic prowess that appealed to a very large portion of the total, male and female, population.

He had been good in sports, tending to favor swimming and gymnastics, a combination which had held him in good stead as far as body development. His exquisite musculature gave him superb anatomical symmetry without the distorting bulk that made weight-lifters seem out of proportion when dressed. His body, combined with his rugged facial handsomeness, made him an excellent candidate for any advertisement requiring a macho man, and attracted more than any man's fair share of women and men.

He finished drying and dressed in clean clothes, gathering up his bloody discards—shoes and socks, raincoat and gloves—in a black-plastic garbage bag which he hauled down to his car. He drove to a secluded spot in the warehouse district along the East River. One by one, he removed the items from the bag and dropped them into the murky water, following them with the bag itself. He got back in his car and drove back to his apartment.

He sat in his dark living room and waited. He fantasized the police banging at his door and calling out for him to give up without a fight. At the same time, the cops, even had they gotten to Pam's room before the CIA cleanup crew, wouldn't have been able to track him down quite yet, even though there was no lack of his fingerprints around the room, including on the murder weapon. He had changed his name and identity hundreds of times since he'd been Sergeant David Mollin, stationed with the U.S. Army in Afghanistan.

At exactly midnight, he picked up his suddenly ringing phone.

"Turn on the local news broadcast," the voice on the other end told him and disconnected. He recognized the voice as Cal Sanders. That the TV coverage was of a specific apartment building awash in cleansing flames said it all. The CIA cleanup crew had taken care of one of Cort's problems, and Cal Sanders was no longer obligated.

That off his mind, Cort turned off the TV and sank back into the silence and darkness of the room. Mentally, he went through a check list of all the other people who owed him favors. Not just anybody would do for what Cort required. It had to be a pro. Once Cort successfully isolated people who might fit the bill, he eliminated them, one by one, as…missing in action… dead…last heard of parachuted into Russia…training guerrillas in El Salvador....

He didn't have the time to look for someone halfway around the world. He needed someone, here and now.

Suddenly, he remembered Larry Passor.

CHAPTER TWO

"YOU KNOW, I'm still finding this God-awfully hard to believe, don't you?" Roger Lenic said, accepting the Chevas Regal on the rocks and eyeing Terrence Flag who had given him the drink. "You want to tell me, again, that I'm not imagining it?"

"You're not imagining it," Terrence said with a laugh that attractively dimpled both his cheeks. At thirty-two, he was an exceptionally handsome man, possessing the kind of almost too perfect good looks that made him verge on pretty. It was only the scar on his left cheek, disappeared into his dimple when he smiled, that saved him from being downright beautiful. His deep blue eyes and classical features further contributed to the package. "I've been persuaded to leave all of the Grey Area excitement behind me for this," he said, giving a motion that included the whole room. "I've become mellowed by the prospect of making just as much money as I have been making all along, only doing it in a more visible and less clandestine arena."

"You been mellowed by love," Roger said. "Where is the sexy bastard, by the way?"

Although Roger hadn't yet met Brad Nelson, he automatically knew the young man would be sexy. Terrence Flag wasn't the type who would have chucked his livelihood as a freelance Grey Area agent for a New York City executive office and some just-ordinary lover.

"Unfortunately, he's been held over in Rome," Terrence said with obvious regret; one, that Brad wasn't near; two, that Brad wasn't going to meet Roger after all.

"Sure you're not keeping him in the wings for fear I'll move in and steal him, and all these plush surroundings, right out from under you?" Roger asked with a teasing smile, taking another swallow of his Scotch. The liquor burned all of the way down.

"If I thought for one minute you weren't as straight as a stick, damned right I'd keep him away from you, and vice versa," Terrence said. "I certainly couldn't risk him with someone as studly as you, if you were gay in the bargain."

Roger laughed, as usual finding it strange that he had somehow managed to strike up such a lasting friendship with a man who was gay and had never made any bones about it from the very first day they had found themselves on the same assignment. Maybe it had all somehow happened because Roger had taken so long really to believe that Terrence *was* gay. Oh, the guy certainly had the good looks that might have made him suspect, but he seemed to have been in the wrong business, at the time, for a homosexual. Faggots, as far as Roger had always suspected, then, wouldn't willingly be involved in the kind of rough and tumble games in which Roger and his cohorts were involved. Roger had, of course, since been forced to discard that particular misconception and archaic prejudice.

"If I can't have you, then, I don't want any other man to have you, either," Terrence said, going to sit behind his large desk. He looked the epitome of an ivy-league graduate who had made it to the top of the corporate ladder through friends of his family. In fact, Terrence's father *had* been well-placed within the business community and had sent Terrence to Princeton. Terrence's father had died of a heart attack, though, brought on by a business crisis, and Terrence had decided he didn't want to follow in his father's corporate footsteps. It was ironic, therefore, that he had, shortly thereafter, allowed himself to be drawn into a profession that would give its participants even more heart attacks if they only lived long enough to have them.

Actually, Roger was happier than hell that Terrence was getting out of the Grey Area. Not only because he could be happy that his friend had found love, but because Roger and Terrence were still friends, and, this way, could stay that way. The freelance espionage game wasn't one that spawned too many lasting relationships, especially for independent Grey-Area operators in their constant flux from one side to the other that so often saw potential friends suddenly on opposite sides. By some remarkable stroke of good fortune, Roger and Terrence had never been forced to come up against each other, and, now, they never would. That gave Roger a good deal of inner satisfaction. Now, if Roger's only other friend, in the Grey Area's free-lance community, Evan Callen, would just find himself some nice safe niche, out of the action, Roger would be completely content with his life as he was living it.

The desk buzzer buzzed; it was Terrence's secretary who said a Mr. Gramlin was calling on line one. Terrence looked at Roger, shrugging an expression that indicated he hadn't the foggiest notion who Mr. Gramlin might be; he told his secretary to tell Mr. Gramlin to try again later. "Say I'm in conference or something," he instructed.

He sat back in his chair and went on with the small talk and light banter, he and Roger reminiscing about old times. They had a supper date for later, Terrence having offered Roger the use of his near-by suite to freshen up. Roger could have gone on ahead, but since Terrence's workday was almost complete, he'd decided to hang around.

"I'm expecting just one final call," Terrence had explained, glancing at his wristwatch. "As soon as it comes, though, I'll chuck everything else."

"Obviously the call you were expecting wasn't from Mr. Gramlin," Roger said. His glass was empty, and he got up, walking to the wet bar.

"While you're at it, do me the pleasure of filling this pretty near its rim, will you?" Terrence said, tossing Roger his glass. Remarkably, the crystal arrived at Roger's end of the toss with its ice cubes still inside.

When Roger brought Terrence the requested refill, Terrence's face was screwed up in contemplative thought.

"Gramlin?" Terrence muttered to himself, following up by taking a large mouthful of his fresh Scotch. "You know, that suddenly does kind of ring a bell." He pushed the intercom that connected him to his secretary on the outside desk. "Mrs. Lipton?"

Mrs. Lipton was an elderly lady who really looked a little out of place in a business bringing profits from recording stars often less than a quarter her age. But, Mrs. Lipton, beneath her prim exterior, knew the record business from top to bottom, having once been a relatively successful singer in her own right, back in the days when rock became more than a stone, and roll became more than a bun eaten with a meal. Terrence had confessed to Roger that the woman was invaluable, and he had no intentions of replacing her with some young man who would have had a jealous Brad chomping at the bit.

Mrs. Lipton said that Mr. Gramlin had left no number where he could be reached. He *had* said he would call again tomorrow.

"Damned if I don't know that name from somewhere," Terrence said, tuning out the reception desk. "Christian name: *Cort*, I think. Did you know him?"

"Should I?" Roger couldn't recall any Cort Gramlin specifically to mind.

"I think he was active somewhere on the periphery while I was helping shepherd Dr. Dleichitz out of Poland," Terrence informed.

"I didn't even know you had a part in any of that," Roger admitted. It had reportedly been a hairy undertaking. Dleichitz was imprisoned at Walonz at the time, his wife and three kids under house arrest. Everyone had been yanked out, though, without a hitch.

"Cort Gramlin?" Terrence repeated curiously. "Nah, it couldn't be him, could it?"

Roger shrugged; he didn't have a clue.

"Think maybe he's left the espionage racket and has started up his own rock band?" Terrence asked and laughed.

"I think it would be safer to assume this is an entirely other Gramlin," Roger said, certainly less able than Terrence to come up with any reason why an old acquaintance in the espionage business might decide to look Terrence up, the Dleichitz thing having taken place ages ago; unless, of course, Gramlin had an ongoing assignment on which he was hoping Terrence would join him. No chance of that, happening, now, though, thank God!

A few minutes later, the call arrived that Terrence was waiting for. After which, the office was left in Mrs. Lipton's competent care; Terrence and Roger headed for the suite Terrence shared with Brad Nelson.

"Nice!" Roger commented as Terrence took him on the grand tour, ending at the wet bar that took up one whole corner of the sunken living room.

"Yeah, not bad," Terrence admitted. "Drink up, and I'll show you the bathroom, complete with a sauna. I'd even join you in taking one, but having you naked in the same room has always been almost too much for this poor straight guy to bear."

Roger laughed aloud, and, then, showered. While taking the few brief steps to the sauna, he heard a distant phone ring and be answered. He opened the sauna, stepped inside, and let the heat engulf him.

When finally dressed, Roger joined Terrence in the living room. Immediately, he recognized something about Terrence that suddenly put him on the alert.

"Anything wrong?" he asked.

"Wrong?" Terrence asked. "Jesus, what could be wrong?"

Through the rest of the evening, though, despite Terrence's evident show of good humor, Roger couldn't shake the feeling that there was *something* wrong that Terrence wasn't telling him.

CHAPTER THREE

EVAN CALLEN CALLED from Seattle. Roger always enjoyed hearing from his now-only-remaining friend in the Grey-Area independent-agent espionage business; this time no exception—at least at the outset.

"I just got off a job that leaves me so flush with excess cash, I've decided to take it easy for a couple of months," Evan said. "You have anything going that would keep you from joining me for a little rest and relaxation on this side of the Continental Divide?"

Roger and Evan had met during a seminar conducted by an organization regularly advertised in *Soldier of Fortune Magazine*. The company made a point of seeing that any man who wanted could be kept up to date about the latest weaponry, self-defense techniques, and anything else that might put bonus points on the side of survival in any field where survival was preferable to the other alternatives. It was another miracle in Roger's life, in his business, where friendships were looked upon to be avoided like the plague, that he had bonded with Evan, as well as with Terrence Flag. Despite all odds, this friendship had endured, re-enforced over the years by short vacations they somehow managed, together.

"Your timing is perfect!" Roger said. "I'm free at the moment."

"Eureka!" Evan exclaimed. "When can you get your ass out here?"

"Three days soon enough?"

"Just let me know your plane flight," Evan said. "We'll meet you."

Roger didn't miss the plural pronoun, and his sudden lack of immediate response indicated as much.

"Roger?" Evan asked, suddenly sounding nervous.

"I'm here," Roger said, wondering why he felt suddenly so down. Was it because he knew what Evan would be saying next, and, on top of Terrence having recently found Brad Nelson, Roger didn't know if he really wanted to hear whatever it was Evan had to say. Was Roger feeling envy? Well, it wasn't as if he actually begrudged Evan or Terrence happiness. Hell, he wasn't shit enough to do that. But, there was no denying that he was just a little jealous if both of his friends had suddenly filled their lives with what was missing from his. If he had somehow had the fortitude to keep romance out of his profession, as it *should* have been kept out of it, then, he was a little resentful that his two best friends hadn't been able to do the same. Oh, it was possibly different as far as Terrence was concerned, in that, at least, he had jettisoned the espionage business at the same time he took on a lover; Roger somehow couldn't imagine Evan quite so willing to do the same.

"I've someone I want you to meet," Evan said, pretty much confirming Roger's worst fears.

"Congratulations," Roger said, not meaning it. He couldn't imagine Evan out of the Grey-Area business, and that meant bad times for whomever his lady friend might be. Damn, Evan should have thought of that, too. A man in love seldom performed as well as one who wasn't in love, and there was something about staying alive in the spy business that was usually compromised whenever anyone's responsibilities suddenly included loved ones.

"You will still come, won't you, Roger?" Evan asked, intuitively having sensed Roger's condemnation.

"Sure, I'll come," Roger said finally. If Evan was going to be saved from a major mistake in his life, Roger would have to do it close-up, not over some long-distance phone line.

"Great!"

Roger no sooner hung up than Terrence called.

"I need a drink, a little companionship, and an alibi," Terrence said. "Want to volunteer for all three?"

"Say when."

"The Oak Room in an hour?"

"I'll be there."

"And, read page ten of this evening's paper, will you?" Terrence said. "It'll give us something to talk about."

Anything in particular?" Roger asked, but Terrence had already rung off.

He read page ten of the evening paper and headed for the Oak Room. Terrence was already there, at a corner table, and nursing a Scotch on the rocks. There was a pause in their greetings while Roger ordered a drink of his own.

"All right, buddy," Roger said, settling back in his chair. "I do believe the next move is yours."

"You saw page ten of the paper?"

"I did."

"And, you still have no idea why you're here?"

"Something to do with the body found in the East River?" Roger suggested. At first glance, he had been a little uncertain what he was supposed to weed out of the large selection found on page ten. When he'd completed his perusal, he'd found the body the only thing that stood out, probably because his business was bodies, and he had deposited more than his share of them in that same river.

"The body is Howard Cahn," Terrence said, although the recovered corpse had simply been labeled "unidentified man" by the press. "He was a termination."

"Consider my look one of surprise," Roger said, having remained relatively poker-faced only because he'd been trained to keep all emotions low-key. "After all, I was just assured, only a few days ago, was I not, that you'd given up terminations for love and a roster of recording artists?"

His drink arrived, making for a slight interruption in the

conversation.

"I did it as a favor for a friend," Terrence said, once the waiter was gone.

"For Cort Gramlin, you mean?" Roger ventured. There had been something about that evening Roger spent with Terrence that put Cort Gramlin in a position of prominence in Roger's memory. Roger had a feel for these things.

"Actually, it was less a favor for him than it was for Larry Passor."

"Passor?" Now, that was name that *did* definitely ring a few bells for Roger, although he'd not heard of Passor for years.

"He saved my life once," Terrence said. "I owed him."

"Do I look confused?" Roger asked; he might possibly put the pieces together if he put his mind to it, but he suspected Terrence was going to do that for him.

"Passor's life, in turn, once saved by Cort Gramlin," Terrence said. "Gramlin decided to call in his note, and I was offered up by default, because Passor got a bullet in his spine a few months back and isn't up to taking on much of anything, these days, let alone terminations. This one really a piece of cake, all the footwork and planning done, and done well, by Gramlin, ahead of time."

"Who wasn't doing it, himself, for what reason?"

"Due to his trigger finger inadvertently slammed in a car door. He went so far as to unwind his bandage to provide evidence he wasn't kidding."

"So, you did the job, and there were problems?" Roger ventured. He wasn't yet sure where this was leading. There was no question that Terrence had taken on the termination; there was no question that Terrence had completed it. And, there was a body, apparently unidentified by the police.

"No problem with the job itself," Terrence said. "The poor bastard didn't know what hit him. I've seldom had anything work so smoothly. The set-up by Gramlin was perfect."

"Which brings us to what?"

"To Brad having shown up early from Rome, my having

never made it home that evening, because I was on the job," Terrence said. "He's jealous, did I tell you?"

"This problem, to which you refer, then, is merely a family matter?" Roger was relieved.

"Hardly *merely.* I told Brad I was reminiscing with you; you and I got drunk; I passed out on the couch in your hotel room. I've talked about you enough, so that he knows you're straight and not a threat."

"You just need me to back up your on-my-couch story, then? That's it?"

"If and when, although even that might not be necessary, in that he says he believes me, and I believe he believes me. However, I do think it's wise to clue you in, just in case."

"No problem," Roger said, finishing off his drink and motioning for another round.

CHAPTER FOUR

SHE SMELLED of *Nosferatu Ilume* by Jfay, which conjured memories of someone, although Cort Gramlin couldn't remember who. Not Pam. Pam's fragrances had been simple, less exotic—roses, carnations. That's one of the things he had liked about her. Now, however, forewarned, he felt safer in the presence of *Nosteratu Ilume*.

She had taken the bar stool next to him. He could tell, just by looking, that she was a working girl but of a better class than usually turned up in this particular establishment. There wasn't anything cheap about her, including her perfume. Her dress was revealing, without being vulgar; basic black with a plunging neckline that showed just enough impressive cleavage to entice without overkill.

She had blonde hair, and a lot of it. It and her large green eyes were probably her best features. Her nose was a little too snub, her lips a little too full. No denying, though, that she looked good. She looked *really* good. And, Cort was horny.

She ordered a martini, very dry. Cort paid for it. She didn't make any fuss about accepting his largesse, either, which Cort liked. He hated the types who were obviously out to turn tricks but still managed, somehow, to get all insulted when easily spotted. She smiled at him over the rim of her glass. She had white teeth that looked as if she might have bedded a good orthodontist at one time or another.

"Hi," she said. She had a low, husky voice that came out in sexy whisper. "You here to get laid, too?"

"Yeah," he said, wondering if she'd spotted his hard-on in his pants. It had been there, of course, before she sat down; her presence only made it harder. He needed a tight pussy to fuck. So what if his need was based on how the last woman he'd nailed had turned on him, and he was out to prove, tonight, that Pam's betrayal hadn't taken the old starch out of his pecker?

"My name is Sally," she said, taking another swallow of her drink and flashing another radiant smile. "You look like a Cal."

"You got the *C* right. It's Cort."

"You look like a Cort," she said with her low and sexy laugh. "Is it true all Cort's have big balls and the very long-handled 'rackets' to go with them?"

"Not this one," Cort said; it was best to get any such expectations on her part out of the way. With his good looks and hunky body, it would have been a little too much of a good thing to have had the good Lord give him a gargantuan cock, as well. Still, that wasn't to say that his dick was all that small, except, of course, when fear shriveled it all of the way into concealment within his pubic hair, as had happened the night he murdered Pam.

"Good," Sally said, licking her lips enticingly. "My pussy is really tight, you know? And, the really big boys can sometimes make a chore out of fucking it, when it should be pleasurable for the both of us. Your cock, I'm presuming, isn't presently supporting the same kind of bandage as your hand."

"It was just my hand, not my dick, which got caught in the car door," he said. "So, how much money are we talking, doll?" He didn't have to look any further for what he wanted. If Sally's pillow talk wasn't likely to include her quoting Jung and Kierkegaard, like Pam had sometimes done, at least Sally wasn't likely to try shooting him dead while he slept, either.

"You have a C-note you're willing to part with for a good time, Cort?" Sally asked. "If not, I could maybe negotiate, just for you."

"I just happen to have one on me," Cort said. Hell, he had more than one. He was really well set, financially, after Terrence Flag had come to his rescue as far as the Howard Cahn termination. Jesus, but that had worked out perfectly. Flag had handled it just like the pro he was, just like Larry Passor said he would. So far, all the possibly bad repercussions that could have resulted from the night of Pam's murder hadn't.

"You want to finish your drink, or get a fresh one at my place?" Sally asked; her tongue was back to making wetter her lips which were already glossy from lipstick.

Cort picked up his glass and emptied it. "Seems I no longer have a drink, here," he said.

Sally laughed and emptied hers. "Ditto," she said, sliding off the stool in his direction and rubbing against him as she did. "Besides, my personal stash of booze is better than this rot-gut."

They walked to her to her place, which was close. Like her, her apartment was a step or two above what usually hosted one of Cort's one-night stands. She was right, too, in that her booze *was* better than what they'd had at the bar.

Her bedroom didn't look like a whorehouse, either. There wasn't a red light in sight, although there were enough dimmers to keep whatever light there was at a bare minimum.

"You sit there." Sally motioned Cort into a chair by the bed. "I'll slip into something a lot more comfortable."

He sat and nursed his drink, watching her step out of her high heels and kick them under the edge of the bed. She went to a chest-of-drawers, opening the top drawer.

"You like black lace, stud?" she asked, pulling out a skimpy, diaphanous pair of baby-dolls, "or shall I move down a few more drawers and pull out my leathers?"

"I like black lace just fine," he said; his left hand adjusted the hard-on still straining at his crotch.

"Yeah, that's what I thought," Sally said. "And to be truthful, I like a man who likes his women looking like women instead of like butch Amazons. You're my kind of man, Cort. You sure as hell are."

She reached behind her back and expertly unfastened the descending row of buttons that allowed her to shrug her creamy white shoulders out of clinging material that dropped around her ankles. One foot stepped out of the pile, and the other lifted the discarded dress so she could reach it and place it over the back of a nearby chair.

She was wearing a sexy, half-cup, black brassiere that hardly contained her large breasts. As far as Cort could tell, so far, there was nothing fake or phony about her. What she advertised was apparently just what the customer got.

She unfastened her half slip and stepped out of it, wearing black panties and a garter belt that clipped the hugging tops of her sheer, black nylons. It was a sight that made Cort even more hot and bothered. He couldn't remember the last time, outside a fuck movie, or a peep-show flick, that he'd actually seen a woman in stockings and a garter belt. Too many of them had moved on to more convenient pantyhose which would never have the sex appeal of garter belts and stockings—at least as far as Cort was concerned. Quite frankly, he would have almost been content to let her stay dressed, just the way she was, saying to hell with the black-lace baby-dolls; except, she would be shedding more clothes to get on that skimpy nighty. While some women lost all of their mystery once they were stripped bare of all the trappings, Cort somehow doubted that was going to be the case with Sally. He wanted her naked. He wanted to see that bush of natural blonde hair at the vee of her legs that was now muted by the silky stretch of her panties' crotch.

Her brassiere came off with the expertise of a stripper, revealing her tits large, firm, and perky, in their entire rosy-nippled splendor. No revealed sag to her buttocks, or belly, as her panties fell away.

"Jesus, Jesus, Jesus!" Cort said; Pam had never gotten him *this* hot and horny. What in the hell had he ever seen in Pam, anyway?

Sally dropped the lacy baby-doll top over her head and worked her arms into its sleeves. The lacy material draped to a point that almost, but not quite, covered the pubic bush that confirmed she was no beauty-shop blonde but the real thing.

She moved to put on the lacy bottoms, but Cort told her not to bother.

"You'll just have to take them right off again," he told her, putting his glass on the nearby table and coming to his feet. Animal impulses inside of him had reached the point where sitting was no longer possible.

Sally tossed the bottoms to one side, prepared to give Cort whatever he wanted—at least for the moment. She walked sexily over to him, running her right index finger down the bit of bare chest revealed by his open collar.

"What say to our making you a little more comfortable, too?" she suggested, unbuttoning the next button of his shirt and moving right on down. Certainly, Cort wasn't about to put up any protest. He wanted his clothes off as much as Sally did.

"Ohhhhh!" she said in appreciation of Cort's revealed chest. She ran her fingers up over his pectorals to his shoulders, moving his shirt off over his arms. "You must spend an awfully lot of your time in the gym, honey?"

"I want to spend an awfully lot of my time *in* you," he told her, knowing that slow and easy preliminaries might make for better sex but he was more and more eager to get down to the humping nitty-gritty.

"Well, it's only going to be a matter of seconds before you get your wish, isn't it?" she said, playfully. Gracefully, she dropped to her knees, her hands down around Cort's ass and along the backs of his legs. His crotch at her eye level, she brought her hands around his hips and began unbuckling his belt.

"That's what I want, baby," Cort readily agreed, excited as all hell and getting more so by the second. "You obviously can read my mind."

She found the tab of his zipper and pulled it down, parting bronze-colored miniature metal teeth. She reached into the breach and took hold.

The force of the bullet entering him from behind sent him forward over Sally who maintained a tight hold on his hard-on until his momentum forced her to let go. He was dead before his head hit the floor, leaving a surprised and disheveled Sally coming up for air.

"Decided to start early, did you, bitch?" Paula Choir said, standing in the open bedroom doorway. The silencer on her revolver was hot to the touch after the kill-bullet's exit.

"Well, he did seem just a little too good to waste, without trying him on for size, first," Sally said. Cort's sprawl kept her on the floor, although she managed a sitting position. It really hadn't taken her long to figure out all that had happened was merely what was scheduled to happen, only earlier. Sally had genuinely hoped to find out if Cort was as good in bed as she suspected he would be.

"You are a slut!" Paula accused; jealousy sparking in her dark brown eyes and in the tightly wound sound of her voice.

"Can I help it if I like a man occasionally?" Sally asked in mock innocence. "I mean, until you manage a permanent dick the likes of which I had hold of in Mr. Gramlin's pants..."

"You're disgusting!" Paula insisted.

"Nah, just horny," Sally contradicted. Her legs butterflied at her knees, the tops of her baby-dolls hoisted above her waist. "And, since you've taken Mr. Gramlin, here, out of play, what say to you and I doing a little something?"

"You think I'm going to step right in and substitute when you've already insinuated I'll be nothing but second best?" Paula asked, feeling that weird feeling in her gut she always did when she saw Sally decked out in black lace and waiting. Certainly, Paula didn't approve of the sexual draw Sally exerted on her, but there was no denying its existence.

"What I should do," Paula said, holding her gun so its long and phallic silencer was more obvious, "is push this deep inside your cunt and pull off the goddamned trigger?"

"Oh, come on, Paula, don't be mad," Sally coaxed, not really fearing Paula's threats. Sure, Paula had blasted Gramlin away without a question. One, Paula hated men. Two, killing Gramlin had been a job. Paula shoot Sally, her business associate, her lover? Sally thought not, and, she was right.

Paula laid the gun to one side, hurriedly slipped off her clothes and joined Sally on the floor. Cort, eyes open and staring, didn't see a goddamned thing.

CHAPTER FIVE

"JESUS, IT'S HAPPENING!" Hank Hesse exclaimed, watching the commotion Sam Hall caused in the shopping mall.

"Come on!" Stephen Milan said, leading the way toward Hall who, after the latter's series of blood-chilling screams, and collapse, had started jerking on the floor like an epileptic in grand-mal seizure.

Unceremoniously, the two men pushed their way through the gathering crowd of onlookers. Still in shock, most of the bystanders hadn't the faintest idea what to do. Stephen and Hank had the advantage of having been forewarned. There was no possible way, after the fit commenced, though, that Hall could be allowed to fall into the hands of hospital or police authorities. It would have involved too many additional people brought into the cover-up.

"Excuse me, please, I'm a doctor," Stephen lied his way through the ever-thickening crowd, Hank in his wake. "Please, let me through. Please."

Hank took charge of Hall's jerking legs, holding them secure. Stephen took control of the rocking head, prying open the downed man's mouth and placing a ball-point pen lengthways across lower teeth. The maneuver, used to keep epileptics from choking on their tongues, wasn't going to do Hall any good, in the long run, but, at least, it looked medically sound, even if the man's bite cracked the pen lengthwise.

"This man has to be taken to a hospital!" Stephen announced. "My car is just outside. Someone give me a hand!"

"Sure!" Hank replied on cue.

"Should he be moved, though?" one woman within the circle asked. "I've always heard...."

"Lady, I'm a doctor!" Stephen challenged; his voice was enough to cow anyone who wasn't positive of correct procedure. "If we don't get him to a hospital and damned fast, he's going to die. Now, can a couple more of you help, here, please?"

"Sure, doc," one of the mall's security police said, figuring a doctor's decision held precedence over anything he'd ever learned in first-aid. "Toby!" he called, bringing another security officer into play. The four hefted the still spasming Hall and carried him through electronically activated doors to the parking lot.

"There's my car!" Stephen instructed, steering the other three, Sam in between, over to the parked vehicle. He opened the back door and helped push Hall inside. Hank got in, too, keeping the man's spasms from jerking them both onto the floor.

Stephen prayed there was no real doctor anywhere in the wings, preparing to rush over to diagnose how dangerous it was to be lugging a sick man around like a sack of potatoes. Stephen didn't really know how Hall should be handled, medically. Their instructions had been to terminate, not save the bastard for later. Any mercy Stephen and Hank showed, now, resulted from their not having managed the termination before Hall went into attention-getting convulsions.

"You want one of us to ride along with you, doc?" Toby asked.

"No, we'll manage, thanks" Stephen said, wanting out of this as quickly as possible. The last thing needed was extra baggage along for the ride. That would require yet another elimination; Hall was headed for no hospital of which these security cops had ever heard. "He's calming, which is a good sign."

In fact, it was a bad sign, by the looks of how the bastard was foaming at the mouth like a rabid dog, his eyes rolled back so there was nothing to be seen but white!

"Want us to radio for a police escort?" Toby volunteered.

"No, the worst is over," Stephen said. Finally behind the

wheel, speaking to the guards through the open window, he started the car and put it in gear. "He really looks far worse than he is. If he goes into another major convulsion, I'll stop and give him a shot of methodonalade." Stephen didn't have the foggiest if there even was such a med, or for what in the hell purpose it would be used. He certainly didn't have any handy.

"Thanks for everything, doc!" Toby said, his companion echoing that sentiment. They were happy as hell that somebody was there to take charge of a situation that was anything but pleasant.

"Jesus!" Hank breathed from the backseat when the car moved out of the parking lot and into mainstream traffic on the street. "Is this shit catching?"

"They say no," Stephen said, reaffirming what Hank already knew. Hank merely wanted reassurance. They had both worked with their U.S. government employer long enough to know that lies were told. Just because they were informed this thing possessing Hall wasn't going to possess them, via physical contact with him, didn't mean shit! Stephen, like Hank, only hoped the reassurances had been valid; if this malady was in the least communicable, the epidemic had surely begun.

"Christ, Stephen, the bastard is starting up again!" Hank said and tried his best to control the renewed flopping.

"Do us and the bastard a favor, and put him out of his misery!" Stephen said. "Just wait until it's clear on all sides." He angled the car for a freeway access ramp that put them on a less crowded throughway, without the hindrance of stop lights. Hall, jerking like some out-of-whack mechanical doll, would obviously bring attention if ever the car stopped.

Hank knew exactly what to do, sliding a knife blade expertly through Hall's ribs for as quick a death as possible. Hank prided himself on his ability to put most men away without much muss, fuss, and/or bother; also, without too much mess. He was an exterminator, not a butcher. If he preferred a knife to any other means of dispatch, with its disadvantage of usually requiring an up close and personal with the victim, Hank hardly muffed any first try.

"Done!" he said, closing Hall's eyes and leaning the man's head into the corner of the backseat to give the illusion of sleep, rather than death. He used the end of Hall's tie to wipe foam-flecks from the corpse's lips and blood from his knife blade.

CHAPTER SIX

"THAT BROAD GIVES me the fucking willies!" Hank said, watching the car exit the warehouse whose door slid closed behind it.

"Yeah," Stephen agreed. "She does give the impression that she'd just as soon see us dead as that poor sucker, there, doesn't she?"

Cort Gramlin's body was laid out on the cold cement floor, partially wrapped in the body bag which had been peeled open for identification purposes.

"You think she and the blonde are banging pussies?" Hank asked, wondering what it would be like to see those two broads going at it in bed, or even his joining on in. Oh, he knew all about watching lesbians in X-rated movies, but seeing them do it in real life, actually participating with them, would have been a real turn-on.

"Why ask me?" Stephen asked with a shrug, although he thought the answer to Hank's question was an obvious affirmative. "Why didn't you ask the dear ladies while they were here?"

"Maybe because I was afraid the dark one … what was her name? Paula Sing-song?"

"Sing-song?"

"Choir. I was afraid she'd take insult and slice off my nuts."

"No big loss!" Stephen said with a chuckle.

"I know quite a few women who might argue that point," Hank boasted, flashing a wide grin.

"Yeah, but they'd have no trouble adjusting by substituting a foot-long dildo with rubber balls."

"Nah, it wouldn't be nearly the same," Hank argued. "If you think so, it's no wonder you're always such a big disappointment to the ladies."

"Yeah, and who in the hell told you I was such a disappointment with the ladies?" Stephen challenged.

Oh, Louise, Mary, Harriet, Joyce, Myra...."

"Ah-ha!" Stephen interrupted. "I don't even know a Myra."

"Well, I do," Hank said. "And, I prefer her company to you or to that of this stiff; so, what say we get this piece of dead meat into its hole so I can check with Myra to see if she really meant it when she said you were a rotten fuck."

Stephen laughed, unable to keep from it. Hank and he went to squat beside the body bag in order to get the corpse back into complete concealment where any smell of decay would be less evident.

"When do you suppose this happened?" Stephen asked, indicating the protective splint on Gramlin's right index finger visible, along with arm and hand, through the partially opened bag.

"It matters, does it?" Hank asked. He hadn't been kidding about wanting to get to Myra. There, now, was a little lady who could show any man, Hank in particular, a really good time!

"It matters a helluva lot if it's been there very long," Stephen said. Unhindered by sexual fantasies, regarding what Hank planned to do with some woman in some bathtub, he was better able to reason possible complications. "If his finger was injured in the scuffle with the girls, I doubt they'd have bothered fixing it for the body-delivery to us, do you?"

"So, he hurt his goddamned finger," Hank said. "Who the hell cares? Certainly, he doesn't. He ain't hurting *anywhere* any longer."

"He took out Howard Cahn," Stephen reminded, not about to be veered from his present line of thought. While Hank was an A-okay guy to work with, he wasn't the sharpest knife in the drawer.

"So?"

"With a gun."

"So?"

"So, is he right-handed?" Stephen asked.

"You want to get to the point?" Hank replied. "It would sure save me a helluva lot of brain work."

"I couldn't pull a trigger with my finger in a splint like that. Could you?"

"Christ, Stephen, who gives a flying fuck if the bastard used his big toe? He got the job done, didn't he?"

"Did he? Did you know that his apartment was watched the night of the termination?" Stephen asked. "He wasn't seen coming out until the next morning. He had some people worrying he *hadn't* completed the job. When Cahn turned up dead, it was just figured Gramlin had a bolt-hole out of his apartment that no one had spotted."

"Who told you that?" Hank asked. He hadn't heard any of it.

"What if Gramlin didn't kill Cahn?" Stephen suggested.

"Come on," Hank replied, a little slow, still, on the uptake. "Cahn is dead, isn't he? If Gramlin didn't do it, who did?"

"Someone Gramlin hired, maybe?" Stephen ventured. "Someone he had to round up at the last minute because of a bum finger? Someone to whom he spilled a bit more about the termination than he should have?"

"Come on, Stephen, don't make a goddamned mountain out of a molehill! You don't even know the bastard wasn't left-handed."

"Maybe I'd better make a phone call to find out, huh?" Stephen said, coming to his feet.

"Suit yourself," Hank said with an accompanying sigh, intuitively sensing that Myra and his sexually slipping and sliding in the bathtub was going to be delayed for far longer than he'd anticipated just a few moments before.

CHAPTER SEVEN

"IT'S A JOB right up your alley," Stephen said, sitting across the table from Roger Lenic; the noise and crowd on all sides assured privacy rather than detracted from it. "A pro like you can carry it off, in nothing flat."

"Actually, I was planning a few days rest on the west coast," Roger said.

Stephen, however, knew Roger's plans weren't set in stone, or the Grey-Zone agent wouldn't have agreed to the meet in the first place. It had to have been obvious, when Stephen called, that it was a job offer he had in mind.

"You can take care of this in no time," Stephen assured, "and still head off for your vacation. Granted your vacation may be a few days late in getting started, but you'll be a helluva lot richer for the delay." He quoted the price affixed to the proposed extermination.

"That's pretty substantial for a *simple* wack-job," Roger said suspiciously.

Stephen shrugged. "I'm just the middleman." He'd told those jackasses there were standard fees for standard kills, and they weren't going to accomplish shit, only suspicion, by offering more for a kill than what the kill should have warranted. The bastards, though, were desperate and showed their desperation, and that was coming back to bite Stephen on the ass. Having lost track of this intended victim for years, only recently having run him to ground, they wanted him taken out quickly. "These guys we're dealing with, this go-round, don't do this sort of thing very often." A lie, for sure. "If they're overpaying…." No lie! "…it's their cost of doing business, and a bonus for you and for me."

"Who's the target?" Roger asked. It wouldn't hurt to get a few more specifics—if he could have them. He'd promised Evan to join him in Seattle, but Roger had more and more second thoughts about doing that now that he knew for certain that Evan was serious about some woman. Any meet-up with Evan at this juncture, was bound to be strained, since the two friends knew romance had no place in their business. It was hardly fair to any woman (or man) to go from newly-wed to husband-newly-dead, all within a very short time span. This was probably just what Roger would tell Evan, too, which would likely cause bad feelings. Hell, maybe it wasn't his place or his business to tell Evan how to run his life. The man had surely made all of the arguments Roger could raise, and, hearing them rehashed probably wouldn't change anything. On the other hand, if Evan called on Roger for a meet-up because he needed someone to talk him out of his foolishness….

"Bruce Franklin," Stephen said, reaching into his briefcase at his feet and pulling out the file. He handed it across the table to Roger who opened it. What was immediately visible was a picture of a fairly chubby man with gray hair, gray mustache, and glasses.

"Franklin is in electronics," Stephen said, duplicating data Roger's quick glance of the typed page had already obtained. "A company called Electon-Max. The company is a big one, always landing government contracts that make the financial pages." Stephen couldn't help being amused that the one man who had escaped detection, all of these years, had been right under their goddamned noses. Not only was he with Electon-Max, but he was living in the same city as had Howard Cahn.

"I presume there's a big contract up for bid?" Roger said. Having been involved in this business enough years, he could deduce certain things from certain things.

"Hardly all that big a contract, as far as Electon-Max is

concerned," Stephen said, reciting his line of bullshit by rote. "Big enough, however, as far as any other company would figure it."

"Franklin dead will shift the balance how?"

"He's keyly placed," Stephen said, which, conveniently, wasn't a lie. "His death will initiate an inner-company power struggle, plus a plunge of company stock points on the exchange. Way too much turmoil for many company people to pay too much attention to one contract falling through the cracks and going elsewhere."

"It's dead they want Franklin, not just laid up in some hospital?"

"There's no doubt but that they want him dead," Stephen said, anxious that there be no misunderstanding of that. The last thing his superiors wanted was Franklin alive, wounded or not, in some hospital.

Roger shrugged. Actually, he preferred killing to wounding or maiming. It was easier to kill a man than fart around trying to manage either of the other two. However, for the money offered for what, so far, showed evidence of a simple elimination, Roger still kept expecting some kind of ball thrown at him from left field.

"So, are there any other guidelines, besides they want Franklin dead?"

"Only the time element," Stephen said. "It's imperative it be done this week."

"That's cutting it a little short, isn't it?" Roger asked, curiously. Usually, he could expect a bit more time to do his pre-kill planning.

"Brought about by constant wavering, among certain people, as regards their guilt for murder versus their greed for profits," Stephen said. In fact, the delay resulted simply because it hadn't been until two days before that Franklin's true identity and whereabouts were known. Had those been known sooner, arrangements would certainly have been made sooner, based upon them. Cort Gramlin had had a month to plot Howard

Cahn's demise, and that termination wasn't any more difficult than this one. "In the end, greed won out," Stephen added. "Considering the apparent lack of complications, I foresee no real problems for a pro like you. Franklin, after all, doesn't have a bodyguard. He doesn't drive a car with bulletproof glass. He's never had any previous attempts made on his life, so he'll hardly be expecting this one."

"No termination is easy!" Roger said, knowing that for the lie it was. However, had it been easy for everyone to kill, people like Stephen would be out there doing it, instead of just brokering deals to make it happen.

"I was speaking comparatively, of course," Stephen said, getting the message and out to salve Roger's possibly wounded professional pride. "For some people, murder is quite out of the question."

"Just let me run what you're proposing by us one more time to make sure I have it correctly," Roger said after a brief pause. "Kill Bruce Franklin. It makes no matter how, just as long as it's done by the end of this week."

"Correct," Stephen said, knowing there *should* have been other instructions...like what to do if Franklin suddenly was dropped by convulsions at any time prior to his assassination? However, there were other people supposedly assigned to deal with that—if and when. If it would be more ideal to have Roger watch for that possible occurrence, too, that would have required him having more information than most thought best to give him. Roger wouldn't have been brought in at all had there been enough agents in-house to carry out all of the terminations required within the suddenly narrowed timetable. Stephen could only hope that the premature seizures of Sam Hall were the rare exceptions. "Oh, yes, I guess there is one more thing," Stephen added.

Roger waited, all along having anticipated that there was more to warrant such an exceptional pay-check.

"These people would like to know when it will happen, so they can make suitable arrangements for alibis, and probably do some insider trading. I've assured them that shouldn't be a problem."

The request wasn't all that unusual in corporate assassinations. No way would a purchaser want himself, or herself, accidently without an alibi at the time of the murder.

"No problem," Roger agreed.

"You'll take the job, then?"

"Sure."

Once back at his apartment, Roger called Evan Callan in Seattle, explaining something had come up, and he would be a few days late. Evan sounded relieved to hear it.

CHAPTER EIGHT

"NO," DR. DICKY DWASP SAID. "That man is definitely not one of my patients.

"Look again!" Stephen instructed. "And, while you're at it, look at this, too." He tossed the bulged legal-size envelope onto the desk top. "It might refresh your memory."

Dr. Dwasp picked up the envelope, folded back its flap, and saw the money inside. He laid the envelope and money back on his desk, beside the snapshot of Cort Gramlin which Stephen had put there.

"I'm sorry," he said. "I really do wish I could help."

"There's going to be no offers of more money," Stephen said. "Don't make the mistake of thinking there will be. All other additional enticements are going to be far less attractive."

"What can I say?" Dr. Dwasp asked, giving the impression that he would like to help but helping was quite beyond him.

"Look, doctor," Stephen said, knowing Hank Hesse, standing guard at the door, but feet away, was growing impatient. The physician was going to regret any interrogation by Hank. "It's not as if we're here to have you reveal some kind of confidence, is it? All we need from you are two simple answers. One, did you treat the man in the picture for an injured right index finger? Two, if so, *when*? Now, for those two simple answers, considering you'll certainly not be in violation of any professional ethic, you should be more than happy to make a few bucks. I know you medical people are swimming in Medicaid money, these days, but surely a little extra, come this easily, is frosting on the cake?"

"What about this man's finger?" Dr. Dwasp asked. He'd been paid for years to repair the wounds of Cort Gramlin and others like him, getting paid for his silence as well as for his services. He found it ironic that his day of reckoning was in regard to a simple finger fracture, when he'd doctored some really nasty wounds in his time.

"Why don't you just let us ask the questions?" Stephen suggested. "You just, please, oblige us with answers?"

"Yes, I put the splint on that man's finger," Dr. Dwasp said, acutely aware of Hank's constantly nervous fidgeting by the door.

"When?" Stephen asked, and the good doctor told him.

CHAPTER NINE

GEROLD LINDSEY HADN'T had time really to enjoy his promotion. Oh, he'd had a few brief days where he'd basked in the glory of having struggled up through the ranks, miraculously surviving, with no loss to limb or sanity, to reach where he was. But, then, the shit had hit the fan.

Firstly, there was the sudden death of his predecessor, Bentley Castle, of a coronary. Granted, it hadn't come as any big surprise. Bentley had been noticeably ill for at least six months before he finally threw in the towel and requested a release. It would just have been nice, though, if he'd hung on just a little longer, after that, in his new role as advisor. There were certain nuances of life at the tip-top that Bentley could have passed on to Gerold, like how Bentley would have dealt with the mess resulting from Project ABABA at Aberlene.

"Here's the poop on ABABA at Aberlene," Bentley *had* said, during one of the meetings when he'd handed over the reins. Bentley's need "to get the hell out of Dodge," left Gerold, in retrospect, wondering if the man hadn't suspected shit would soon hit the fan. "It's pretty much inactive, except for our monitors. I doubt you're going to have to worry about it, since most of its participants have already died of old age."

The problem turned out to be those few remaining who were suddenly dying of *other than* old age, ABABA suddenly no longer inactive. Gerold, within the tip-top echelon, had the resulting mess dumped right in his lap, along with the realization that any kind of leak to the press would likely topple him from his perch like Humpty Dumpty from the wall. And, like old Humpty, there would be no putting Gerold—and a helluva lot of his associates—back together again.

It made no difference that ABABA was initiated at the facility in Aberlene, Pennsylvania, at a time when Gerold was still a kid, and that it had come to a virtual standstill before he was ever recruited as a U.S. intelligent agent.

Jesus, why did it have to happen to go active on his watch? If it had to burst its shitty bubble, why not when Bentley was still in charge? Hell, Bentley, sick anyway, and ready to leave, ready to die, could have survived a tarnished reputation better than Gerold. But, oh, no, it waited not only until Gerold would get full blame but until Bentley was dead and buried so Gerold couldn't even use him as an advisor (let alone as a convenient scapegoat).

It was unthinkable that anything about ABABA at Aberlene should/could leak! People wouldn't understand, even after all of these years. Gerold wasn't sure even he understood, although there was no way he admitted that, even to himself. He was a team player and had loyalties to uphold. His job, in the end, wasn't to condone or condemn decisions made by others, before him, over whom he'd never had any control. His job was simply to keep this under wraps until it could fade into oblivion.

Thank God, unexpected death, number one, Deke Fread, had occurred on that man's fishing trip in the Cascades.

Luckily, Stephen Milan was the agent who'd been watch-dogging Fread. He had seen Fread go down in the stream, and he had gone into the water to rescue him. Fread, however, had been beyond rescuing. And, Milan had handled everything exceedingly well. Thank God for men, like Milan, cool enough to analyze a situation, and competently do what he had to do. So far, smart men had been in the right places at the right times to keep repercussions of ABABA pulled from the brink. The only thing that had Gerold worried was that not all agents had as much going for them as Milan who had, once again, luckily been there to handle the ABABA-related death of Sam Hall, as well as the clean-up after the Cort Gramlin termination, and, more recently, in arranging for the termination of Bruce Franklin. The only reason Gerold was able to include Hank Hesse in his list was because Hesse was partnered with Milan; the former definitely with the brains of that duo; Hesse, left on his own, would probably totally fuck up.

Gerold sat behind his desk and told himself to get a grip. Things might yet work; certain things might yet fade into blessed obscurity. Except if they did fade, he would still be faced with finishing up the cover-up of the cover-up. How many men had he consented to have murdered to conceal the long ago activities of ABABA at Aberlene?

"God, help me through this goddamned mess!" he said aloud; his manicured fingernails tapped nervously on his desktop.

Ten other ABABA participants seemed likely to follow in Fread and Hall's death-throe footsteps. Bruce Franklin had just been re-added to that list, after having been out of sight for over twenty years. Somewhere along the line, Franklin had simply, inadvertently, faded from the grid. Someone, possibly thinking ABABA genuinely dead in the water, and putting out only piss-poor effort to locate Franklin, once Franklin was lost, had, either purposely, or inadvertently, marked him "deceased." When, in fact, Franklin wasn't deceased, even if he soon would be, and was one more ticking time bomb who, unless defused—hit by a car, wiped out by a mugger, drowned in a boating accident, buried in the fallout of Mt. St. Helens (or some other obliging volcano), or officially terminated—might provide the key for some clever layman to unlock skeletons that Gerold's career required be kept securely locked away.

Gerold frankly preferred that, if destined for failure, it had been obvious from the get-go. It didn't seem fair if he was able to bring things almost to a successful conclusion, only, then, to have them blow up in his face.

Definitely, there were complications in Gerold not having nearly enough people he could trust. If only he possessed an endless army men as faithful as Milan, then, it would all have been so much easier. As it was, though, he was likely surrounded by more than one "somebody" who wouldn't blink an eye while passing on state secrets, or leaking defamatory evidence of ABABA to the press. Among the latter group, there were always do-gooders who somehow managed to survive, despite all efforts to willow them out, or win them over. Gerold found himself with only a very few people upon whom he could truly rely, and in whom he could confide *all* the ABABA at Aberlene details. There was another special few to whom he was able to give *some* details. To those two groups went the task of farming out the wet work to those other independent Grey-Area agents who hadn't a clue as to the why they were paid to kill who they were killing. This resulted in killers killing and, in turn, being killed, in order to cover ABABA tracks, and muddy Aberlene waters. All part and parcel of a very dangerous game that Gerold, knock on wood, seemed to be winning, at least for the moment.

He was startled by the buzzer on his desk that, although not intended as a reminder, reminded that he could use another Valium.

"Stephen Milan to see you," his secretary informed. The arrival of Milan might have brought Gerold some relief, were he capable of thinking more positively, these days. Continued suspicion, though, that his luck had about run out, made him nauseatingly suspicious that Milan was bringing bad news. What's more, he was right. Still, things might have been worse, in that Milan, as usual, seemed to have everything well in hand.

"I'll take care of this termination personally," Stephen said, "assisted, with your go-ahead, by Hank Hesse who's always ideal if a job needs to be done cleanly."

This additional termination, tacked onto the others, was necessitated by events which, if Gerold could believe, originated with a goddamned injured index finger—for Christ's sake!

Cort Gramlin, professional assassin, hired to kill one of the people, Howard Cahn, on Gerold's hit list, had apparently injured his trigger finger. The injury had necessitated Gramlin probably bringing in another freelance agent, Larry Passor to do the job for him. When Gerold thought of how easily Milan might have overlooked the splint on Gramlin's dead-man's finger, he got chills up and down his spine, as well as a sick feeling in the pit of his belly.

According to Milan, all evidence pointed to Passor having been recruited by Gramlin, if just because, at the time of his finger injury, Gramlin was reported looking for Passor. Since Gramlin had once saved Passor's life, Milan assumed that IOU was called in. The reasoning was logical. While Passor had since dropped out of sight, Milan had a contact who thought he knew where Passor was. As soon as that was confirmed, Milan would terminate Passor.

"Of course, we can't be sure what information Gramlin passed on to Passor, if any, since Gramlin really shouldn't have known all that much to pass," Stephen reminded, "but, as it has been standard operating procedure, up until now, to eliminate those hired to eliminate, I assume that still applies?"

"Yes, I think you're right," Gerold readily agreed. What was one more murder at this stage of the game? The more securely he plugged even the *potential* for leaks, the better off, and safer off, he and the all-important ABABA at Aberlene secrets were going to be. He could count on Stephen Milan and Hank Hesse for a clean kill. Now, if he could just have the elimination of the three remaining ABABA subjects as easily accomplished and as efficiently dealt with as Passor.

Bruce Franklin still had to be killed, right there in the city. Karen Caffner still had to be killed, in Rome. Lenox Pratt still had to be killed, in Seattle. Those three, plus the three people hired to kill them, equaled six murders.

Goddamn, Gerold was going to be glad when this *was* all over and done.

CHAPTER TEN

EVAN CALLEN CHECKED the bullets in the clip of his automatic, feeling strangely excited doing what he was doing. He had actually thought, there for awhile, that he might give up this life, having met Arden, convinced that he loved her and, therefore, equally convinced that the stimulation of committing murder was no longer something he needed. He'd been wrong in both assumptions, of course.

Affirmation of his growing suspicion that he'd been a fool to think himself ready for love and retirement had occurred during the sudden silence force-fed him by his old friend Roger Lenic, from the other end of a cross-country telephone line.

Yes, Roger knew the truth, no ifs ands or buts, and his condemnation of Evan's stupidity had come across without any needed speech. It must have taken all of Roger's willpower to keep from saying what he wanted to say. Roger, though, always a smart cookie, had kept silent for fear Evan truly believed his life of adventure was over and done because of some woman.

Evan's present target had originally been scheduled for elimination by an agent unexpectedly pushed off the Space Needle by someone out to settle an old score. Evan was brought in to carry on with the termination needing to be done before week's-end. All supposedly to do (who ever really knew?) with the victim, Lenox Pratt, being about to make a new will; his son, present chief beneficiary, about to be disinherited. Time of the essence.

Originally, Evan rationalized his acceptance as just a case of money too easily made to pass up. Later, though, even he recognized that it wasn't the money as much as the excitement he derived in the lead-up to the kill, the kill, and the aftermath of the kill, none of it ever duplicated by however many times he humped Arden senseless and made her squeal and squirm beneath him.

He had been temporarily saved the bother and eat-crow embarrassment of informing Roger of Evan's decision to dump Arden and revert to professional killer, by Roger having called to postpone their intended few days together. Evan preferred breaking the news to Roger over drinks, on a face-to-face basis, when it would come across as the good joke it was, to be enjoyed by every both men, except, of course, not by Arden who had never had the faintest notion that Evan killed people for a living and that he had every intention to keep on killing them.

Evan and Roger were cast from the same mold, except Roger had apparently better adapted, in that Evan couldn't imagine Roger ever calling to confide how he had finally found the "love of some little woman" to edge him into retirement. Not that Roger didn't like women. Hell, Evan and he had fucked whores silly, a few times in the same bed. Roger, though, unlike Evan, wouldn't, for even a New York minute, ever indulge the fantasy that he preferred the high of fucking cunt to the high of committing murder.

Evan put his automatic weapon into his shoulder hostler and turned to the file folder on the table, even though he had the dossier picture and its data pretty much committed to memory. Lenox Pratt was a chubby, gray haired little man, with glasses. He worked for West Coast International Hotels and was in Seattle for a seminar of hotel bigwigs. He would be killed that evening while getting into a taxi, after he had eaten a late supper at a restaurant six blocks from his hotel.

CHAPER ELEVEN

THEY KILLED LARRY PASSOR, really having little choice in the matter, although killing the poor bastard, in his wheelchair, hadn't been one of Stephen's finer moments.

It wasn't only the killing that left a bitter taste in Stephen's mouth but the torturing of the poor cripple, the latter of which Stephen had pretty much left up to Hank Hesse.

"Fucking bastard put up a fight to the very end, didn't he?" Hank observed, wiping sweaty palms on his pants legs. "Had I been in his sorry position, even before we arrived on the scene, I would have welcomed somebody showing up to offer me a way out."

"Well, we got what we came for," Stephen reminded; the end hopefully justified the means.

"You don't suppose this Terrence Flag, who Prosser brought in, passed it on to somebody else, do you?" Hank asked. "I mean, we might end up spending the rest of our lives killing off people, never getting to the bugger who really blew Howard Cahn away."

"Intuition tells me we can stop with Flag," Stephen said, knowing that the trail he'd set out to follow, since the splint found on Cort' Gramlin's trigger finger, couldn't likely extend much farther, "if just because of the time-line; Howard Cahn, after all, died on schedule."

CHAPTER TWELVE

"COME ON, HONEY, it happens to every man at one time or another," Lena Queenlin consoled, sitting up in bed and propping a large pillow behind her for support. The sheet slipped to reveal her more than ample breasts which came complete with dollar-size nipples.

"Yes, well, this is only the first time it's ever happened to me!" Gerold Lindsey said, receiving very little comfort from Lena's diplomatic attempts to soothe his battered masculine psyche.

What he *really* meant was that this was the only time it had happened to him *with Lena*; just going to show how ABABA had gotten to him. Certainly, it had happened plenty of times to him in bed with his wife, Darla. But, hell, Darla didn't have the equipment with which to work that she had when Gerold had first bedded her on assignment in Berlin. Their cover, at the time, required they masquerade as husband and wife. The charade was so pleasurable for them that they'd decided to make the marriage a reality. Holy matrimony, of course, had, also, resulted because Gerold and Darla met at the right place at the right time. He had just received word that he was transferred to the desk job that would groom him for their intelligence agency's top slot; Darla had contemplated leaving her position for over a year and jumped at the chance to do her fade-out via becoming the wife of someone so obviously on the organization's fast track.

God, Darla had been beautiful! Now, however, her breasts

sagged, and so did her tummy and ass. If Gerold was unable, on occasion, to perform sex with her, he rationalized it was the direct result of his no longer being turned on by her.

When he couldn't get his cock up for Lena, though…well, *that* was another kettle of fish. She came with all the right stuff to make any eunuch's prick go hard as a nail. Gerold had never seen a woman who could lay claim to "having it all" until she arrived, one day, somehow, as his good luck would have it, assigned to his staff.

"Here," she said, reaching for both wine glasses on the bedside stand. The wine bottle was there, too, couched in a silver ice bucket. "You probably just need a few more minutes of relaxation."

"Sure," Gerold said, taking the glass she handed over. He sampled the admittedly excellent wine, remembering all he'd ever heard about alcohol as a sexual depressant.

"I know this is probably something I shouldn't say," Lena said, eyeing him over the rim of her glass. She made no attempts to cover her bare breast. She knew they, on a body with a lot to brag about, were her two best features. Also, she knew that if she could successfully maneuver Gerold over this little sexual bump in the road, she'd likely have him right where she wanted him. "Sometimes, it really does help to talk things through."

"What 'things'?" Gerold asked, draining his wine and extending his empty glass for a refill. At the office lately, ABABA was all he *did* talk about. Every time he thought he saw an end to it, something else turned up. Now, there was someone in the mix called Terrence Flag who Larry Passor had possibly brought in on the assassination of Howard Cahn, as a favor to Cort Gramlin. Well, Gramlin was now dead, so was Passor, and so was Cahn. Would the termination of Flag finally plug all of the holes once and for all? Gerold certainly hoped so.

Actually, he should have been more confident of success, now, than before. He was certainly far better off today than he had been when he had suddenly been faced with each and every remaining ABABA subject needing to be terminated, one of those having been missing. Now, there was only Lenox Pratt needing extermination in Seattle, soon to be terminated by an independent Grey-Area agent, Evan Callen; Bruce Franklin soon to be put out of his potential misery by independent Grey-Area agent, Roger Lenic. After that, only Callen and Lenic needed to be dealt with. A definite chance for conclusion on the horizon, Gerold's sexual problem was probably just the result of his gut feeling that something else was just bound to go wrong.

"I know, in your position, you have a lot of top-secret things on your mind," Lena said. Having refilled Gerold's glass, she now refilled hers. "I, also, know that you've probably been worried, time and time again, about how bedroom conversations are often the least secret talks you can have. Certainly, I wouldn't want to be privy to any information that might later compromise either of us. But, if there is anything you'd like to say, that you *can* say, rest assured that I'll never take it any further than this room." Not that she could make any such promises about the tape recorder specially built into the bed.

"Thanks, my dear," Gerold said, leaning to put his lips onto the nipple of her left breast. He gave a noisy suck, wondering if he were really feeling any responsive swelling at his crotch, or whether he was merely indulging wishful thinking. He decided it was the latter, and he pulled away for another swallow of wine. "I'm afraid strain is simply the burden I bear, in the position I'm in."

"Well, consider my offer a standing one," Lena said, knowing she couldn't afford to be pushy at this stage, no matter how anxious she and her associates were to find out just what was going on. Undeniably, there was something in the air, and that something had been there for quite some time. No matter how tightly the lid was kept being kept on it, and the lid had certainly been kept tightly enough on this baby, there was a certain sense of "something", much as the aroma of cooking almost always escaped any covered pot or pan. That, so far, it was only aroma said a good deal about extensive keep-the-lid-on-at-all-costs precautions being taken.

"Thanks," Gerold said, finishing off his glass which he handed to Lena. She went through the pantomime of asking if he wanted more to drink. He shook his head no. As he did so, he mentally computed the dangers in suddenly just opening up to Lena and spilling his guts about ABABA and why it so bothered him to the point of having brought him to impotence. It wasn't as if Lena were some two-bit hooker he had picked up on a binge, someone who couldn't be expected to keep her mouth shut. She was a vetted member in good standing of his little organization. She had a security clearance. If that clearance wasn't nearly as high as that required for those presently involved in cleaning up ABABA, well, then, Gerold still doubted she would have any real problems getting any such required security upgrade. Gerold really would have liked unloading on someone who really wasn't as intricately involved as he and the others were. Lena, so far removed, might have made an excellent sounding board. Then, again, there were already too many people brought in by sheer necessity, without adding to the list one more just because Gerold suspected doing so might put a bit of starch back in his limp pecker.

Would Lena be a non-condemning ear, anyway? That was certainly something to be considered. Oh, she was certainly a bona-fide member of the organization, aware there were often authorized terminations, but how would she respond to so many of them to cover up a project initiated clandestinely so many years before? How would she react to the purpose behind ABABA in the first place?

"I've had enough wine, too," Lena said, putting her now empty glass to one side. "Why don't you let me take a few minutes to see if I can't fix what's wrong with you via some other way besides chit-chat?"

She scooted down in the bed, pulling the covers with her to unveil the non-responding cause of Gerold's present condition.

"Baby, I really don't think even you are going to be able to do much good this evening," Gerold said. It was an admission he really would have preferred not making.

Nor did Lena succeed in doing much good. However, she did give it the old college try, and Gerold appreciated how she never made any derogatory inference to his flagging manhood. She merely continued to maintain her very good act that things like this happened, at one time or another, to every man she'd ever bedded.

"It never stopped a one from coming back later, either, with a resurrected dick, to fuck me silly," she said, realizing that not even her expertise was going to perform any miracles on this cock, at least tonight. "It's not going to stop you, either, stud. You just wait and see."

Gerold only hoped she knew what she was talking about.

CHAPTER THIRTEEN

THE HIGH-POWERED DUM-DUM bullet took off half Bruce Franklin's head and splattered it and his brain all over the white evening gown his wife was wearing when the couple got out of the car to preen momentarily before entering the theater. There would later be a letter that would inform the police and the press that the killing was committed by members of "Heirs of Hiroshima", a group pledged to rid society of all capitalistic pigs who insisted upon keeping the world in constant war by manufacturing weaponry. "Electon-Max is one such weapons manufacturer of which Bruce Franklin was a chief spokesman," said their letter. After which, actually no more than a fictitious group conjured for the convenience of the real assassin, Roger Lenic, the group faded into complete oblivion.

Within seconds of Franklin's head, or at least half of it, being disconnected from his body, Roger had the murder weapon dismantled, packed in its carrying case, and with him along the escape route he'd mapped out beforehand. A short hour later, the weapon was dropped into a foundation form destined for filling with concrete the very next morning as part of yet another high-rise complex being raised over the city, and Roger was in his apartment, wiping up the remnants of the masturbation he'd performed to relieve some of the tension the evening's activities had built up inside of him.

When the telephone rang, he had a Scotch in hand.

"Roger, this is Brad Nelson," the voice said from the other end of the line. It was a low, masculine voice that Roger had little difficulty attributing to the young man he knew was the lover of his friend, Terrence Flag, although Roger had still never met him.

"Hey, Brad, how are you?" Roger asked, sitting the edge of the couch and taking another sip of liquor. "Terrence has told me so much about you; I feel I know you."

"I'm calling about Terrence," Brad said. "Would he happen to be there with you?"

"Here?" Roger asked, stalling. Suddenly, he felt placed in a ticklish predicament, not knowing whether he should tell the truth, or a lie; the latter in hopes of somehow protecting his friend. "He's not here, Brad," he said, suddenly realizing that Terrence would surely, like the last time, have had the sense to clue him in if Terrence had needed an alibi of any kind.

"I was afraid of that," Brad said, his voice strange.

"Are you two having trouble?" Roger asked, thinking that a logical possibility.

There was a pause, a long pause, one that had Roger nervous enough to interrupt.

"Brad, are you there?"

"Listen, do you suppose you could come over?" Brad asked. "I have to talk to someone, and I'm not too sure who else to turn to but you, since I think Terrence is in some kind of major trouble."

"What kind of trouble?" Roger laid his glass on a nearby table, no longer thirsty.

"It's really not anything I think I should talk about over the phone," Brad said. "Actually, I'm not quite sure it's something I should be discussing under any circumstances, but, frankly, I'm worried shitless. Terrence was supposed to meet me yesterday for lunch, and he never showed. He didn't show last night, or today, either. It's not like him to drop out of sight without some kind of explanation.

"You two have a…." He was going to say…"lovers' quarrel", but he changed his mind. "…fight of some kind?"

"Nothing like that," Brad assured. "I think it has something to do with a job he was on, recently. Not a music-related job, either, if you get my drift."

"Yes, I think, maybe, I do," Roger said, figuring he understood only too well. "I'll be right over."

He picked up his car keys from the dresser in the bedroom and locked the door when leaving. He buzzed for an elevator that seemed to take forever to reach his floor. Finally, though, it did arrive, its doors did open. He stepped inside, the doors closing behind him. It began its slow descent, and the explosion rocked the building.

CHAPTER FOURTEEN

WHAT THE HELL? Did they think he was a fucking fool? Well, if they thought that—and they obviously did—he sure as hell fooled them. Evan Callen was nobody's idiot. He had been in his line of business too goddamned long not to have anticipated the trap in his bedroom.

The dead man on the floor, made Evan genuinely angry that his enemies thought they were going to take Evan out, he none the wiser.

Before dying, the dead man had inadvertently provided a whole gamut of leads, including his name, Hank Hesse.

Had Hesse successfully killed Evan, rather than vice versa, there would have been less chance of the police ever coming up with the whys and the hows of the Lenox Pratt assassination. Hell, the cops had enough trouble unscrambling even one murder, let alone two that were connected. Had Lenox Pratt's wealth been great enough, his son just might have decided to cover his tracks as completely as possible by having his father's killer killed. If that were the case, the turd was going to be damned sorry he ever put out a contract on Evan Callen, because Evan wasn't a goddamned novice who didn't watch out for the pitfalls of the killing business.

He was disturbed that his state of mind affected his handwriting. Someone else might not have noticed but he did.

Shit, why in the hell did complications have to happen? His kill of Pratt had outwardly appeared one of his easiest. So, why hadn't he, job well-done, been allowed to go off on his merry way? He hadn't made any move to blackmail any of his other clients, in the past, and he wouldn't have tried blackmailing this one. The bastard surely knew that from his past performance record. Certainly, he knew how to cover his trail well enough so the police would never have an inkling of who had hired him for the Pratt killing. Well, the sonofabitch who hired the killer who had tried to kill Evan was soon going to find there was a hell of a lot to fear from Evan still alive.

Evan addressed the larger manila envelope to Snyder Graves and slipped the smaller, addressed to Roger Lenic, inside. The smaller envelope contained the dossier Hesse had given Evan on Lenox Pratt. While it was common procedure to destroy such dossiers, Evan wasn't the only operative who sometimes held on to them as kinds of insurance policies. Any fingerprints on such folders could sometimes incriminate all by themselves. It had been purely luck, though, that he hadn't destroyed this one, since he really hadn't expected such a simple kill to evoke such complications.

Snyder Graves, the addressee on the outside envelope, was an intermediary who could be counted upon to deliver the inside envelope to Roger. Roger could be counted upon to put the file somewhere for safekeeping until Evan had additional need for it.

Evan hadn't the faintest idea how much postage was required. Every time he turned around, the U.S. Postal Service raised its rates. Luckily, he had enough stamps on hand to more than cover whatever would have been chocked up by an official weighing. Since he was going to the post office, he could have been a bit more precise in using it's mail-weighing scales, available in the alcove set aside for night mailings, but he didn't feel like wasting that time, especially since he still had to dispose of Hank Hesse's body now wrapped in a rug and stuffed unceremoniously into the back of Evan's car. Body-stuffing a rug was always turning up in movies, if just because it really did remain one of the most inconspicuous ways of getting a corpse from Point A to Point B.

He tucked the envelope between his belt and his stomach, pulling his coat shut. He went downstairs to his car and drove it to the post office, depositing the envelope in the night drop. He headed south to the slough just south of Seattle. He'd dumped three previous terminations there, none having yet come to light.

On the stretch of freeway passing by Boeing Airfield, his car exploded, splattering him, Hank Hesse, and automobile parts all over the highway and bordering countryside.

CHAPTER FIFTEEN

NERVOUSLY, ROGER WATCHED the well-built young man, looking very college jock, weave through the clutter of tables and lunch-time crowd, after having had Roger's table pointed out by the headwaiter. A good deal of Roger's paranoia was the result of his apartment having just gone up in an orange-red ball of flame, and how he might well have gone up with it if he hadn't been safely in the elevator at the time. It was only his knowing that his enemy wasn't likely to have discovered his whereabouts, quite yet, might even possibly consider him successfully dead, which kept him confident where he was.

"Roger?" Brad Nelson asked upon reaching the table.

"Do sit, please," Roger said.

Brad Nelson looked squeaky clean, all-American boy, with whom any mother would have loved a daughter involved. Did he and Terrence really do all of those things queers were supposed to do in the privacy of their bedrooms?

Brad ordered a Scotch, and Roger simultaneously motioned for another of the same for himself. The waiter faded into the crowd.

"Tell me why you're worried about Terrence?" Roger said. He had half expected Terrence to show up with Brad, rather surprised that he hadn't. Brad had been right in that Terrence wasn't the type to simply disappear into the blue without leaving a trace, at least under the present circumstances. Had Terrence been on a job, in the profession he'd given up for his new one, it would have been one thing, but he'd sworn off his old ways, yet again, after the Howard Cahn termination, and Roger had believed him. Terrence performed the Cahn kill merely because of an old debt owed Larry Passor. Terrence wouldn't have taken on any other jobs which might endanger Brad and his relationship. If he had, it seemed likely he would have covered his ass, using Roger as his alibi, once again, like the time Brad had returned early from Rome. Certainly, Roger hadn't heard anything from him. However, had Terrence tried within the last few hours, there would have been no answer in Roger's bombed-out apartment.

"He hasn't called our condo or the office," Brad said. "I thought you could tell me what he's up to."

"You'll excuse me if I've lost track of your reasoning, somewhere along the line, won't you?" Roger said; a slight uplifting of his right hand warned that the waiter was arriving with their drinks.

Roger ordered a club sandwich. He wasn't hungry, but they were supposedly there for lunch. Brad scanned the menu and ordered an omelet in order to feed the same illusion

Quite aside from the way Brad's butch good looks challenged all the old stereotypes of homosexuality, he, also, challenged the stereotype of "music tycoon." Having seen his share of musicians and their representatives, Roger had trouble placing this clean-cut guy into that loony-tune world. However, Brad was one of the biggest producers in the music business. Three of the singles released under his label were in the top ten, another marked with the bullet that heralded it for big times on the *Billboard* chart.

"Look Roger," Brad said, sitting back in his chair, as soon as the waiter was, again, gone. He folded his arms across his chest and looked Roger unflinchingly straight in the eyes. "I wasn't born yesterday, and I certainly wasn't fool enough to get involved with a stud I met in a gay leather bar without doing a little checking into his background."

That seemed to call for some kind of response from Roger. However, he didn't give one, despite the pregnant pause which

Brad provided.

"Are you suddenly struck dumb, meaning that you want me to spell it out for you?" Brad asked finally. "Give you the facts and the figures, regarding Terrence's involvement in certain activities that might be described as a shade on the other side of the law, if they were ever proved?" He reached into his coat pocket and pulled out five pages of typed paper which had been stapled, and, then, folded lengthwise. He handed them across the table to Roger. "Speculation regarding your own activities begins in the middle of page two," he said.

"Speculation is all it is, too," Roger said, after a quick glance told him that Brad did, indeed, have viable information sources. "There's nothing here that gives concrete proof regarding anything."

"Right you are!" Brad gave ready agreement. "Had there been, I would have dropped Terrence like a hot potato, no matter how excited and horny he gets me in the bedroom. There's enough scandal in my business, the way it is, revolving around sex and drugs, to suddenly have it get around that Brad Nelson is carrying on a gay relationship with a man who trades in government secrets, at the drop of a hat, and who carries a gun that drops men just as easily. I made damned sure he would come across clean, in the end, after however thorough an investigation. I made damned sure he was out of your business and into mine. In short, I worked damned hard to get what I wanted, and I'm a piss-poor loser. If Terrence is gone, now, it has nothing whatsoever to do with me or the music business. This leaves me only with this." He reached back into his coat pocket and pulled out a photograph which he passed across the table to Roger.

Roger got a funny little feeling in the pit of his stomach as he looked down on a fairly chubby face with gray hair and mustache. It was Bruce Franklin, the executive from Electon-Max whom Roger had blown away in front of the theater.

"While I was in Rome," Brad said, filling the silence, "as I think you are likely very much aware, Terrence killed this man as a favor for another man called Larry Passor."

"Killed *this* man?" Roger asked, wondering how Terrence's informants had gotten it so wrong as to confuse Bruce Franklin with the man Terrence murdered. What in the hell was name of the man Terrence said (or, had he even said?), he'd terminated as a repayment to the debt owed Passor?

"The guy in the picture is named Howard Cahn," Brad said, as if he had somehow received Roger's unasked question via mental telepathy.

"I don't think so," Roger said, still trying to fathom the mix-up. Having killed Bruce Franklin, Roger certainly knew exactly who he'd lined up in the sites of his high-powered rifle and blown all over Mrs. Franklin's pretty white dress."

"Oh, but I assure you it is—or was," Brad insisted.

But, then, maybe this *wasn't* Bruce Franklin who Roger was seeing in the photograph, in that there *were* certain differences between the two Then, again, just because this guy wasn't wearing glasses...

"How can you be so sure this is Howard Cahn?" Roger asked, back to believing Brad's sources screwed up, no matter how much other stuff they'd gotten one-hundred percent right.

"Because it's the picture that came with the dossier on Howard Cahn that Terrence was given to prepare for the kill," Brad said.

Roger didn't believe that for one minute.

"This supposed dossier to which you refer," Roger said. "Do you suppose there's a chance I might see the rest of it?"

"Somehow, I anticipated that request," Brad said, taping his stomach with his right forefinger; the resulting sound indicated a file folder beneath his shirt. "I brought it with me. Though God knows, Terrence will probably be furious as hell if he shows up and discovers I've ferreted out his little hiding place."

Roger still refused to believe Brad brought him evidence that pointed toward the man in the picture being Howard Cahn. For sure, the photo was Bruce Franklin who Roger had blown away. Were Cahn and Franklin, possibly, one and the same, Terrence having somehow botched the termination, the reason for his present disappearance; Roger brought in to finish the job?

"I want Terrence back," Brad said. "I want him back more than anything else in the world. But, if that's not possible, if someone has hurt or killed him, I want that person or persons dead. Do you understand? If you find them but can't kill them, for whatever your reasons, you must promise to let me know who they are, and I'll take care of all the necessary arrangements."

"If they've hurt or killed Terrence, and I find them, I won't need any help from you, or from anyone else, in their terminations," Roger promised.

Brad gave him the folder.

CHAPTER SIXTEEN

GEROLD LINDSEY FELT GOOD. Hell, he felt damned good! He'd been so caught up in the successful resurgence of his sexual prowess that he'd completely forgotten that there were still a few ABABA strings left dangling that might yet trip him up. Like, what Evan Callen might have mailed from that Seattle post office the night he died. Like, why Roger Lenic's body hadn't been found in the debris of that man's exploded apartment.

Still, two strings were better than the many which had been hanging only a few days before. Since then, Terrence Flag had been killed, leaving Howard Cahn's death finally so submerged in cover-up that there was little chance that the termination would ever be traced back to Gerold. So, yes, all things considered...

"See, what did I tell you?" Lena Queenlin said, still pressed beneath Gerold's naked and sweaty body and wishing he'd crawl off. Jesus, he was heavy, all dead-weight! He should really lose a few pounds. "You're not only back into the swing of things, but you're even better than you were before. If a short bout of impotency did that for every man, doctors would universally recommend it."

"You're sweet," he said, giving her a wet kiss that did a good deal to replenish his drained excitement. Still, he knew he was too cum-depleted at that moment to make any Superman effort to commence an immediate sexual repeat. He rolled, giving her room to breathe. "I've only you to thank for my you-know-what's resurrection."

This wasn't simply a line of bullshit. Oh, there was no doubt that the trials and tribulations of ABABA had likely been mainly responsible for his sex life temporarily so out of kilter, but, without Lena, his recovery wouldn't have been nearly so speedy. Had he counted on his wife to work the magic, his cock would have still have been useless as a wet noodle. He'd given Darla a try the night before, when he'd felt possibly again on the verge of being able to perform, and she had, as usual, grown cold as a deep-sea cod. He suspected she preferred he lose his virility permanently.

Lena, though, was supportive through the whole goddamned ordeal. If she wasn't so young, if he wasn't so old, if divorce wasn't so goddamned messy, if the resulting scandal wasn't likely to reflect badly on his career, Gerold would divorce Darla and marry Lena in a New York minute. As it was…

"Don't give me credit where credit isn't due," Lena said, reaching for her robe and wrapping it around her bare shoulders. She slipped out of bed. "You and your penis would have come out of your droops with or without me."

This was probably true, except Gerold figured he and his cock had come out of it far faster because of her. He watched her move gracefully across the floor to disappear into the bathroom to do whatever a woman usually did after having had a stud stallion treat her to a rip-roaring cowboy good-time ride.

He stretched, reaching for the headboard, pointing his toes toward the footboard, hearing several of his vertebrae crack. He pulled a corner of the sheet over his crotch, never having enjoyed the small worm-like quality his penis assumed after a good fuck. It always seemed to shrivel into something pitifully small and vulnerable, compared to the robust thrusting-machine it was when erect.

Water ran in the bathroom sink. The toilet flushed. Gerold tried to picture Lena's movements by merely listening to her sounds.

Lena, Lena, lovely Lena! What a high point in his life she

had become. She was the one person he had been with, these last few trying days, with whom he could genuinely feel at ease. His rapport with her, now missing between his wife and him, had something to do with Lena still an active participant in his business; Darla hadn't been for quite sometime. His wife had been anxious to retire, even at the time she'd met Gerold in Berlin. She'd embraced retirement to such an extent that it was hard to imagine she'd ever squeezed off a trigger and blown U.S. enemies to Kingdom-Come.

In contrast, Gerold had became more and more immersed in the nitty-gritty of American intelligence work as he'd risen farther and farther within its ranks toward the substantial position he now occupied within it. His increasing envelopment was no better illustrated than by his degree of commitment to finding a solution to the ABABA problems. If he could be toppled by the scandal, his need for self-preservation was supplemented by motivation driven entirely by his genuine devotion to duty and to the protection of the impressive legacy of the organization for which he worked. What were a few dead people left along the way?

He had grown increasingly resentful of Darla throughout this whole to-do about ABABA, because she expressed not one iota of interest in whatever it was that was so obviously playing havoc with his well-being. Had she kept her high security clearance active over the years, he could have taken her into his confidence, talking over with her the things which bothered him. As mere housewife, she hadn't wanted her security clearance and had let it lapse; Gerold hadn't been able to confide a goddamn job-related thing to her in years.

Well, he had put wheels into motion that wouldn't have him go through another crisis without someone to talk to. He'd put Lena up for a crypto-top-secret clearance. He'd pulled in some favors and asked for a rush job, too, so it wouldn't take all that long to make it happen. After all, she already had top-secret, so he foresaw no difficulty with her upgrade. He planned to make her a present of the new clearance designation, as well as with the promotion that went with it, as her reward for having stood by him.

The bathroom door opened, and Lena glided back across the floor. She removed her robe once she reached the bed, pausing stark naked so that Gerold could feast his eyes on her loveliness. If his penis wasn't returned to complete stiffness quite yet, it was definitely exhibiting all the signs of being there soon.

"I'm glad that trouble you were having is over," Lena said, climbing into bed beside him. Her skin was soft and oh-so-warm.

"What makes you think it's over?" Gerold asked, fishing for another compliment about his returned libido.

"Isn't it?" she asked. She rolled her eyes and gave a little giggle. "There I go, again, doing the very same thing I promised myself, over and over, that I wasn't ever going to do again."

"Which is?" he asked.

"Pry, silly," she said. "After all, what real business is it of mine? Right? Right! I just keep laboring under the illusion that we're ordinary people able to share all things. You're not angry with silly-old-me, are you?"

"Certainly, not," Gerold confessed. "My problems, though they're certainly not all over, are certainly less today than they were yesterday." Hell, there was no real need for him to be so horribly vague. After all, she was a member of his team, and, in just a few days, she would have her crypto-top-secret clearance, and she could be told more details, anyway. "All that remains for me to do is tie up a few loose ends, like a dead man who hasn't yet been found but soon should be, and finding out what was in a letter mailed in a Seattle post office by another man who is also, now, dead."

"That doesn't sound to me as if your problems are over," Lena said, wondering if she really had a chance of making heads or tails out of this. She had begun to believe that she was never going to get Gerold to open up.

"In order to see the difference, you'd have to know what kind of a mess I inherited to begin with," Gerold said. If he was tempted to go into a bit more detail, in order to boast just a little as to how he had so expertly pulled the organization out of the fire, he decided against it, if only because of the decided stirring of his cock beneath the sheet. "Let's not talk, anymore, right now," he said, pulling back the cover to reveal the wonder of his renewed erection conjured by her just for her.

She laid back and opened her legs for it. She would rather have talked than have sex, but she had her foot in the door, now, and had to be extremely careful, lest she get it chopped off before she could get completely inside, or, at least, withdraw safely. Up until now, she had been careful to hide her true interest, and she figured she would be a bloody fool to try and rush things.

"Ohhhh, baby, baby, baby," she moaned, simulating the first of several orgasms she would find herself faking while Gerold progressed from start to finish, with his huffing and puffing atop her.

When he was finally done, was finally dressed, and had finally gone, Lena was left—as usual—sexually frustrated. During a whole evening of sex, she hadn't managed one real orgasm.

She could have masturbated. That was the release mechanism she had regularly used until quite recently. Masturbation never seemed to leave her quite as satisfied anymore, though, as it once had.

Against her better judgment, she called Paula Choir, asking Paula if she would like to come over. Paula was more than happy to oblige. Having recently broken with Sally Taln, Paula found Lena more than an ideal stopgap. The two women had made it together several times before Paula and Sally had become an official "couple", and they were back to doing it again now that Paula and Sally had parted company. Unlike the relationship between Paula and Sally which, while it lasted, had included love, what was between Paula and Lena was nothing more or less than purely unmitigated lust, without any attending emotional ties. Both women, at that time in their lives, found that the ideal situation.

CHAPTER SEVENTEEN

ROGER LENIC WAS UNEASY as the pilot announced that some Montana town was now visible out the window on the left side of the plane. He didn't care about any bird's-eye view of Billings, or maybe the pilot said Butte. Roger couldn't remember. His thoughts immediately returned to where they'd been before the unappreciated interruption. He had never really enjoyed pilots and crews who played tour guides, pointing out each town, mountain, river, and stream etched on the ground below. It had been his apparent misfortune, though, to have gotten one of those fountains of useless information this time around.

He had decided to fly to Seattle for several reasons, not the least of which was how he couldn't help thinking the people out to get him, having missed exploding him with his apartment, would realize their error and find him, more quickly, were he to remain where he was. He had hopes that leaving would see them sniffing out so many cold tracks that they would simply give up, assuming the explosion *had* blown him into so many little bits that there was no chance of them, or anyone else, finding any traces of him ever again.

He still wasn't sure just who "they" were. In the period between his lunch with Brad Nelson and his boarding the plane for Seattle, Roger had called in a lot of old favors-owed in order to obtain several pieces of the puzzle, none of which seemed to give him any kind of complete picture. One of the strangest things to come out of this was how Howard Cahn and Bruce

Franklin *were* two different men, even if their resemblance to one another was so damned freakish that it wasn't any wonder Roger, when seeing Cahn's picture, had confused it with one of Franklin. Hell, those two men could have been twins. If some people believed everyone had a double, somewhere in the big wide world, how strange, still, that both of these look-alikes had been terminated within virtually the same time-line. Granted, Cahn's termination had nothing whatsoever to do with contract bidding by Electon-Max, Cahn having had no connection with that company, but there was something strange about Terrence contracted to kill Cahn, only to end up disappearing so completely after the successful completion of that contract, while Roger was contracted to kill Franklin, and, shortly after successfully accomplishing that, just missed out on becoming a puff of smoke. There was, also, the question of Larry Passor who had brought Terrence in on the Cahn termination. Where in the hell was Passor? He, too, had completely dropped off the grid. Not easily accomplished, one might think, for a guy confined to a wheelchair. If the rumor on the street was that the Cahn assassination had really originated with Cort Gramlin, where in the hell was Gramlin? Roger had certainly heard of him, but there was apparently no finding him, at least at the moment, either. He'd last been reported in a bar on Robinson Street, leaving with some unidentified hooker. Roger would have attempted looking further into that bit of information, but he'd decided to put a little distance between the east coast and him until he, too, became more definitely a member of the growing group *considered* permanently dead and/or permanently missing.

Not that he was feeling any too confident about his decision to pick Seattle as the place to drop out of sight. Oh, it seemed ideal enough at first. He had, after all, already made arrangements to go there. Evan was expecting him, and no one knew he was due, except Evan and, probably, Evan's new girlfriend, Arden; neither of whom was likely to have spread the word, if for no other reason than that there were few people who even knew of Roger's close friendship with Evan. It wasn't something either ever broadcasted. Friendships within any area of spying and espionage made those involved vulnerable to where it was definitely better not to let anyone know there was anyone available about whom they had any kind of feelings, or with whom they had any kind of emotional attachment.

However perfect Roger's idea of fading into the woodwork with Evan and Arden, though, had been tainted by the call Roger made to Evan's apartment the previous evening.

"Inspector Derrickson here," responded the male voice at the other end of the line. Who in the hell was Inspector Derrickson? "Hello?"

"I think I must have the wrong number," Roger said. He would have hung up immediately, but he couldn't remember the last time he'd dialed a wrong number. However, if connected correctly, the presence of Inspector Derrickson foretold possibly ominous circumstances. Roger verbally repeated the number he was sure he'd dialed.

"Who is this, please?" Inspector Derrickson queried; someone in the background said something that Roger couldn't quite catch.

"Is Evan Callen there?" Roger asked, by then thoroughly suspicious. Inspector Derrickson had made no denial that Roger had reached Evan's number.

"Who should I say is calling?" Inspector Derrickson asked.

"Rog," Roger ventured, thinking that was vague enough. How many people called "Rog" were, after all, in the big wide world out there?

"Rog who?" Inspector Derrickson persisted.

"Evan will know," Roger said. "Just tell him I'm on the line, will you, please?"

There was a pause followed by muffled sounds that were the obvious result of something across the phone's mouthpiece.

"I'm sorry, Rog, but Evan is tied up t the moment and would like to know if he can call you back," Inspector Derrickson said shortly. "Is there a number at which you can be reached?"

Roger had hung up. The closer Roger got to Seattle, the more his intuition told him something was wrong there, too. He only hoped he wasn't stepping from the frying pan into the fire.

CHAPTER EIGHTEEN

ROGER TOOK THE limousine from SEATAC airport, and it dropped him directly at the Washington Plaza Hotel where he had a confirmed reservation under the name of "Taylor Crenshaw." Immediately, he tried to call Evan, getting no answer. He showered and shaved and tried Evan's number again; no answer.

He dressed and went downstairs where he rented a car from the girl operating the Hertz booth in the lobby. He had several fake drivers' licenses from which to choose, using the one for Taylor Crenshaw, since the girl asked if he was staying at the Plaza, and he said, yes. If he interpreted her question correctly, it was as much a come-on as it was for information needed for the rental form. Roger, though, didn't take her up on her offer. He had things to do before crawling between the sheets with another stranger. He would, however, keep her in mind for later.

He drove to within a few blocks of Evan's apartment building and got out. Less than an hour later, he figured he had someone else's stakeout staked out. At one o'clock, the man Roger watched was relieved by another man. By two o'clock, not much else had happened. For all Roger knew, the stakeout wasn't even concerned with Evan's apartment but with something entirely different.

He drove back to his hotel and placed another call to Evan, surprised when he got an answer. Not Evan. Not Inspector Derrickson. A woman.

"Arden?" Roger asked, taking a stab in the dark.

"Who is this please?" she asked. Her voice was low and

unsteady.

"It's Rog," he said, figuring he'd already given Inspector Derrickson that much information. Besides, if this were Evan's girlfriend, she'd need his name by which to identify him.

"Roger Lenic?" she asked and started to cry.

"Arden?" Roger wondered what in the hell was up. "Can you tell me where I can reach Evan?"

All he heard was more crying, accompanied by a woman obviously attempting to get her emotions under control.

"He's dead, Roger," Arden managed finally.

"Dead?" Roger was shocked, whether he had expected the worst or not. "How in the hell can he be dead?"

"I tried to call you," Arden said. "I couldn't find your cell number, and the operator kept telling me that your New York City land line was out of order."

"How did it happen, Arden?" Roger persisted.

"His car just blew up," Arden said, her voice breaking. Whatever composure she'd momentarily managed was lost again.

"Don't leave there," Roger instructed. "I'll call you back in a couple of minutes."

He hung up, knowing that if there was someone watching Evan's apartment, there was a very good chance Evan's phone was bugged. There had possibly been a trace out on Roger's call from the moment Arden picked up the receiver.

He went down to the garage and got his car. He drove the city haphazardly for a few minutes and parked.

Immediately, Arden answered the phone, seemingly in better control. Apparently his hang-up had given her time to get somewhat composed.

"For some reason, God only seems to know why, his car just blew," she said.

Roger had déjà-vu, recalling his apartment likewise disappeared in a puff of explosive smoke. Could there be a connection? His friends were disappearing like crazy. Coincidental?"

"They think it as a bomb," Arden said, her voice back to

strained. "Who would have wanted to put a bomb in Evan's car?"

"You have any ideas?" Roger asked; his question brought a small gasp of disbelief from her end of the line.

"I don't think Evan had an enemy in the world," she managed finally.

If Arden truly believed that, then Evan hadn't ever been completely honest with her. Certainly, Evan had enemies. In his business, a guy could gather them like flypaper gathered up flies. Those enemies might very well have the expertise to blow his car and the car's contents.

Roger watched the second hand of his wristwatch, estimating the time needed for at trace. He was going to have to hang up damned fast if he wanted to make sure no trace went through.

"Let's meet," he said. "The Space Needle observation deck in half an hour?"

"How will know it's you?" she asked. A logical question, since Roger doubted Evan had a picture of him. Pictures were anathema in their profession; the fewer the better. The secret to long life was the ability to remain anonymous.

"I'll find you," Roger said. "What are you wearing?"

The quickness of her answer, no further attempts by her to get his description, left him pretty sure she wasn't out to entrap him, like Inspector Derrickson would have had her do.

"Half an hour," he reiterated and hung up. He got the hell out of there. While he figured he still made it under the wire, as far as any trace, he never liked to cut things too close.

He drove the city for a few minutes, checking to make sure he hadn't picked up a tail. As soon as he was confident he was clear, he drove to the fairgrounds left over from a World's Fair that took place in Seattle, at some time or another, and parked the car in the lot.

He didn't buy a ticket for the elevator up the Space Needle—a phallic projection surmounted by saucer-like restaurant that turned to give diners a three-hundred-and-sixty degree view of the area. Instead, he positioned himself off to one side, after buying a hot dog from a nearby concession stand. He pretended to be watching kids in bumper cars ram the shit out of each other. In reality, he was keeping an eye out for Evan's girlfriend.

He knew her the minute he saw her, right down to the big, pink rose in the straw sun hat she was wearing. Considering Seattle, as usual, was on the verge of another downpour, from thick rain clouds, the summer hat was easily spotted in all its incongruousness. Just as easily spotted was the hatless man following the hatted woman. Roger would have pinpointed the tail even without recognizing him as the same fellow Roger had spotted, earlier, standing watch outside Evan's apartment building.

There was no way Roger could now chance a face-to-face with Arden. Unless he wanted to talk to her on the phone, hanging up every few minutes, to avoid a trace, he might well be out of luck, period. Not that he suspected she had anything to offer. He continued to suspect that Evan had left the poor woman pretty much in the dark as to what Evan and Roger did for a living.

He left the fairgrounds and drove to the downtown-branch of the library. He dug through recent issues of the *Seattle Times* until he found RESIDENT KILLED IN FREEWAY CAR BOMBING.

He scanned the short column and found absolutely nothing to tell him anything. Whoever was responsible for planting the bomb was still unknown. So, too, was any motivation for the bombing. Evan Callen, victim, seemed to have no immediate family. The remains of the other man, in the car with him, remained unidentified.

CHAPTER NINETEEN

IN THE VERNACULAR of the intelligence community, Lena Queenlin was a "mole," an official employee of a foreign nation expected to burrow, clandestinely, up through the strata of her U.S. intelligence-agency employer, supplying more and more vital bits of information to her "control" as she progressed. So far, she'd contributed several items of interest, although she had never previously been really pressed to supply much, because it had always been assumed a virtue to wait until Lena achieved the right level on the intelligence ladder to access the right information of far more value than she might have been able to sweep up along the way. When information had been needed, from those lower levels, other avenues had been tapped, unless, of course, as had sometimes been the good luck (albeit, not for the U.S.), Lena had been in position to obtain the needed data without putting any spotlight on herself. There had been times when her handlers thought certain information warranted pressing her for more involvement, but on each of those occasions Zregory Litzen vetoed the suggestion.

Zregory saw big things for Lena, and he refused to risk them by subjecting her to the possibility of early exposure. Lena had skillfully managed to become the mistress of her intelligence agency's chief, Gerold Lindsey, and she had been sending back enticing little tidbits, for the longest time, that hinted something of possibly major importance in the works. That Zregory had put out feelers elsewhere, to other contacts within the same organization, coming up with the big goose egg, left him even more enticed. The absence of leaks, except via Lena, seemed to indicate that whatever was being kept under wraps was good stuff indeed.

It wasn't standard operating procedure for Zregory personally to summon any of his moles for vetting. The less direct contact he had with them, the better it was for all involved. Certainly, there was no way he wanted any suspicion cast on a key mole like Lena.

However, Zregory hadn't gotten where he was by playing entirely by the book. If his methods were sometimes a bit unorthodox, there was little complaint in the face of his stellar record of achieving prime info.

He decided to see Lena, one-on-one, for several reasons, not the least of which was his displeasure at her resumed sexual liaisons with Paula Choir. The first, several years back, had, even then, set Zregory's nerves on edge. There had been nothing in Lena's file to indicate she had lesbian leanings, or Zregory would have been less disposed to nurture her as his special protégé. Not that homosexuality, in men or women, was the problem it had once been, but it still added complication to a business already complicated enough as it was.

He had been exceedingly pleased when Paula had finally taken up with her fellow agent, Sally Taln, especially when Lena hadn't shown any immediate inclinations to take up with any other woman. But, as soon as Paula and Sally split, Lena had gone rushing into the breach. That definitely wasn't advisable, considering the key role Lena began playing the minute she started sharing her boss' bed. Zregory had gone over Gerold Lindsey's dossier on more than one occasion, and didn't think the man was nearly liberal enough in his sexual outlook to accept, any too gracefully, that his own sexual prowess seemingly wasn't enough to satisfy the woman he'd taken as his mistress. Lena had Gerold thinking he was one of the few men who had ever managed to sexually satisfy her, and anything waiting in the wings to shatter that illusion was a danger to Lena's viability as a mole.

Zregory, also, wanted to impress upon Lena that he, personally, was paying particular attention to her progress. No one was ever immune to a bit of flattery from the top, and it usually inspired them to make greater effort and sacrifice. That was exactly what Zregory expected Lena to do for the greater good—provide greater effort, make greater sacrifice. If he had saved her for years, sloughing off other minor information-gathering projects onto others in order to protect the sanctity of her position, he intuitively sensed something in the works, here and now, that finally warranted Lena risking exposure more than had been pressed upon her in the past. Something was going down, and Zregory wanted to know exactly what it was. As he saw it, and he had looked into the matter extensively, his only pipeline for that revelatory data existed within the bedroom relationship of Lena and Gerold. If excerpts of their recorded bedroom conversations offered enticing insight into someone dead whose body was missing, whose body shouldn't have been missing … someone else, before dying, having mailed something unknown to someone unknown from a Seattle post office … those were pieces of a puzzle Zregory meant to solve. If Lena was professing to be doing as best as she could do, Zregory suspected she could and should do much better. What's more, he intended to see that she did.

His summoning of her required far less precaution than would have been necessitated in his summoning someone in a more minor position within the same agency in which Lena was employed. Presently, she was just too high-ranking to have her loyalties seriously questioned. That didn't mean, of course, that Zregory didn't put into place all security procedure when having her picked up at her apartment and delivered to him. He never underestimated the enemy, even if the enemy came off, at times, incredibly stupid, as did Gerold Lindsey in having taken up with Lena Queenlin. The only government officials more easily coaxed into letting their defenses down it the bedroom than Americans were the British. Sometimes, it was hard for Zregory really to have any genuine respect for men so continuously more ruled by their cocks than by their (albeit obviously tiny) brains.

"Lena," he said, standing to greet her. He came around his desk and crossed the thick carpet to reach her. He took her hand and kissed it, giving her the royal treatment. When he finally got around to telling her to get off her damned ass, he wanted her to take it as a request from a high party official who saw in her capabilities she probably missed seeing in herself.

"Sir!" she said, realizing what an unexpected honor it was to be called into Zregory Litzen's presence; she was made a little uneasy by the honor. Any variance from standard operating procedure insinuated something in the works.

"Let's sit over here," Zregory said, guiding her to a section of his office that had the appearance of a formal drawing room. High-backed chairs and a couple of couches were grouped before an attractive marble fireplace with unlit wood piled in preparation for future burning. He motioned her into one of the available chairs, taking the one directly across from her. Between them was a small, glass-topped coffee table centered with a sliver tray of crystal decanters and brandy snifters. "A cognac, my dear?" he asked her, beginning to pour even before she nodded her yes-please assent.

More than a little nervous, she eyed the attractive, elderly man across from her, suspecting that behind the façade of expert tailoring, manicured nails, and gentile courtesy, was the brain behind a good deal of successful clandestine prying into the U.S. intelligence network. What she knew about Zregory would do the Americans little good, though, had they ever gotten hold of her and tried to extract it from her, by whatever means. She couldn't prove Zregory as powerfully placed as she knew he was. In fact, it had been long-time rumored that the Americans suspected his behind-the-scenes nefarious involvements, but they hadn't been unable to trip him up, possibly because he had the assist of diplomatic immunity.

"I want to talk to you about several things, Lena," Zregory said, trying his best to act fatherly. "Let's begin with your boss and lover, Gerold Lindsey." He handed Lena one of the glasses with its hearty measure of expensive cognac. He took another of the glasses for himself and settled back in his chair. "Mr. Lindsey presently has access to some information that I desperately want, and you seem the only person in position to get it for me. You do know, I hope, that I wouldn't personally be calling on you if this wasn't so very extremely important, don't you?"

Lena nodded yes and took a sip of her cognac that burned all of the way down to her belly.

CHAPTER TWENTY

IF ROGER ACCOMPLISHED very little by his trip to Seattle, except provide the increasingly disturbing pain in his gut that resulted in knowing for certain that another friend of his had died, Brad Nelson accomplished a good deal more.

"Money talks," Brad said, seated in one of the antler-horn chairs of the isolated Washington State cabin he'd purchased for his meeting with Roger once Roger had reported in that Seattle was unsafe, "although, I must confess, I've bought pretty much all I can from whomever my sources. You'll have to ferret out the rest, knowing there's more money available if and when you need it."

"So, let's hear what you and your money managed, this time around," Roger said. He was pleased with the meeting site. The cabin was in a well-protected and well-defendable geographical location and had the additional advantage of all the electronic gadgetry, for security, with which Brad had been able to equip it on such short notice. Surprisingly, Roger felt safer, there, than he ever had in Seattle.

Brad drank some Scotch. "Stop me if you've anything to add or subtract."

"Sure."

"Terrence was asked by Larry Passor to take on the killing of Howard Cahn in payment for an old debt Terrence owed Passor. In turn, Passor had likely been approached by Cort Gramlin who originally was contracted for the hit but had suffered a hand injury. When last seen, Gramlin was exiting a bar on Robinson

Street with a supposedly attractive hooker, name unknown. Except, the woman in question wasn't a hooker but Sally Taln, employed by a U.S. government agency so secret it doesn't seem to have an official name; or, so I was informed by a gentleman called Parmer Folds. Does that name ring any bells?"

"No," Roger admitted, thinking this newly purchased information of great interest, indeed. That he'd never heard of Parmer Folds didn't mean squat, in that the chances were very good the informant's real name wasn't Parmer Folds, any more than Roger's real name was Roger Lenic.

"Enticed out of the woodwork by an offer of a substantial sum of money, Folds revealed this interesting tale," Brad continued, obviously pleased with his successful delving. Not that Roger could blame him. Certainly, Brad had come up with something Roger hadn't been able to find. "Folds was out to see Gramlin dead," Brad said. "Something to do with a project in which the two were involved a few years back, on opposite sides. Anyway, to make a long story short, a girl Folds liked— read that, 'loved'—was killed during the operation, for which Folds blamed Gramlin. Folds swore revenge and called upon the services of a woman called Pam Dyne who, as I understand it, had enough physical charms to wheedle her way into Gramlin's confidence. Somehow, though, Gramlin got wise to Dyne and proceeded to take her out, instead of vice versa. At which point, Folds decided to kill Gramlin, sans any other middle-man, or middle-woman. He followed Gramlin, waiting for just the right moment to lower the proverbial boom. Before the right moment arrived, however, Gramlin was picked up by Sally Taln in that bar on Robinson Street. Folds recognized her from a job long over and done. He watched her take Gramlin to her place. Folds followed. Gramlin came out bundled up in a body bag carried by Sally and Sally's fellow agent, Paula Choir. The body was delivered by the two women to two men, in a warehouse. At which time, the men checked the bag's contents, apparently to confirm Gramlin was inside. Folds was, thereby, equally assured of the corpse's identity, albeit from a discreet distance, and didn't bother following the men or the body, content in knowing Gramlin—finally—was dead."

"Are you sure this isn't just some line of bullshit Folds laid on you for cold cash?" Roger asked. He should have known better, by now, though, than to underestimate Brad.

"A friend of mine had him rigged to a polygraph at the time," Brad said. "While such tests aren't always fool-proof, I'd say this one, spontaneous as it was, as far as Folds was concerned, left my friend and me convinced he was telling the truth."

"My recommendation, then," Roger said, "is that we don't waste more valuable resources in farting around but make directly for the one person we now know will likely prove most informative."

"Namely, Sally Taln?" Brad intuited.

"You're sure you're in the music and not a government spook?" Roger was impressed.

"I'm not only in the music business," Brad said, "but I infinitely prefer it to the business you're in. That confession made, I'm still determined to find out what happened to Terrence."

"Not only will we find out," Roger said, "but I promise you that any harm done to him will see those bastards responsible pay." Roger no longer had any doubt that Terrence was dead, probably terminated by the same people behind the deaths of Passor, Gramlin, and Cahn. "Now, about Sally Taln…"

Brad reached into his shirt pocket and pulled out a folded piece of paper. He leaned forward and handed it over.

"Well, it looks as if you've, once again, done your homework," Roger congratulated, "meaning the rest is, as you say, likely best left up to me."

CHAPTER TWENTY-ONE

IT WAS HARD FOR SALLY to be on guard 24/7/52/365. Oh, it was different when she was officially on assignment. Then, she was naturally paranoid even if the assignment classification normally wouldn't warrant her targeted for termination by the enemy. When she was off duty, taking a long-deserved rest, after having wrapped a job run pretty much like clockwork, she hardly expected a pseudo gas man ("Checking the area for a possible leak, ma'am!") to pull out a gun.

There had seemed nothing unusual about Sally opening her door and finding him standing there. Although he was handsomer than hell, there was little that was threatening about him, at least at first glance.

"It's probably nothing, but we're getting hinky gas readings and feel it best to check on them," he said. Admittedly, Sally had all the fantasies any single woman might have as regards any sexy, hunky, utility-service man, suddenly on her doorstep. Unlike Paula Choir, Sally needed a man, on occasion. Sally putting the make on Cort Gramlin, prior to his elimination, though, had been the straw that broke the camel's back, as far as Paula and Sally's relationship, at least as far as Paula was concerned. Paula was such a hopelessly jealous bitch that Sally took a good deal of pleasure in agreeing it was time to cool things between them, at least for awhile. Of course, Sally hadn't planned on Paula so immediately back to bumping pussies with Lena Queenlin. So, Paula was still getting sex every night, while Sally had no one—male or female. It might have been different if she had at least been able to sample Cort Gramlin's dick inside her before Paula blew him away (with a gun, not with Paula's skillful lips). The gas repairman just seemed the best prospect Sally had for sex in a helluva long time.

He had asked her, please ("ma'am"), to see her basement. She opened that door for him, turned on that light for them, and, then, followed him on down. He looked better and better; damned fine viewing from the rear.

What he pulled out, though, wasn't his prepared-to-fire-cum cock but his prepared-to-fire-steel-bullets gun: surprise number one.

Surprise number two: "Why did the people you work for find it necessary to terminate Cort Gramlin?" he asked, just as calmly as you please.

"Beg your pardon?" Sally thought she'd misheard. There was no way any gas utility man, gun or no gun, stood in her basement and asked about the termination of Cort Gramlin which had gone down easily as pie. Sally would have likely already put that elimination out of mind if she hadn't been so close to sampling some of Gramlin's sexual goodness-graciousness before Paula ended all chances of that ever happening.

Utility-man, obviously *not* utility-man, smiled widely, as if they were both enjoying some insiders' joke. However, Sally couldn't afford amusement. Obviously, he wasn't a member of her "in" group, but, still, somehow, was cognizant of classified information. His presence insinuated a leak (and not gas). She planned for her escape; though, she'd likely waited way too long already. She didn't need a score card to know how much advantage he had.

"I don't understand," she said, trying for calm, cool, and collected. It was damned hard when she'd progressed from trying to decide how to seduce him to how to escape and/or kill him. "That isn't a real gun, is it?"

"Would you like me to demonstrate its viability by firing a bullet from it into your kneecap?" His smile widened, as if he really hadn't threatened her at all. Yet, Sally saw something, previously unseen, deep in his eyes, which assured her there suddenly wasn't much inside his handsome exterior, other than cold, hard, unyielding ice.

"I really don't know why you're here," she said, continuing with her bluff; it was all she had.

"Oh, you know, all right," he contradicted. "What's more, whether you know it or not, you're going to tell me everything I want to know that you know."

She was wrong if she thought she could outlast his determination, because she did end up telling him everything, at least as much as she knew; which really wasn't all that much. More importantly, she gave him the name of the one person, outside Gerold Lindsey, who possibly *could* fill in all of the blanks—if anyone, besides Lindsey, ever *could*. There was even undeniable satisfaction she took in implicating Lena Queenlin; she didn't forgive the bitch for being there to pick up the pieces for Paula when Sally said bye-bye. Sally had expected Paula to come running back, begging for forgiveness. Which Paula would have done, too, if Lena hadn't been there to volunteer as stand-in—complete with incredibly tight pussy and incredibly big tits.

CHAPTER TWENTY-TWO

ACTUALLY, IT WAS SOMEWHAT of an afterthought, on Roger's part, done only because he suddenly found himself in the neighborhood, after his termination of Sally Taln had him driving aimlessly around in an effort to await the ebb of his adrenaline rush.

Snyder Graves looked up when Roger entered the shoe shop. He was seated at his desk in the back of the room, as he always seemed seated there whenever Roger stopped by. Snyder doubtfully had ever repaired or shined a single shoe in his entire life. The shop had once belonged to his cobbler father, and Snyder had gone off to Afghanistan to discover more profitable ways of making money than following in daddy's footsteps. As a result, Snyder's presently entire legitimate shoe-repair business had a workforce entirely hired; he devoted himself, full time, to the more lucrative letters, packages, and other deliveries that arrived on his doorstep, addressed on the outside to him, but, invariably, addressed on the inside to the really intended recipient.

"Hi," Roger said, took Snyder's outstretched hand and shook it. "Anything for me?"

"I'm thinking you might have a couple of items waiting," Snyder said. If he'd heard rumors that Roger was dead, killed in a bomb explosion that had made front-page NYC headlines, he'd learned, a long time ago, that one could never put much stock in anything read or heard. Therefore, he acted hardly surprised, and in fact, was hardly surprised, to see Roger suddenly arrived and possibly resurrected. Nor did Snyder ask any questions, figuring, rightly so, that the specifics were none of his business. His business was managing a mail drop, and there wasn't a piece of mail he'd received that he hadn't held onto until the addressee showed up to claim it. He had some pieces which he'd held for over twenty years, refusing—as with Roger—to believe the dead were dead unless he personally saw the bodies; sometimes not even then.

Momentarily, he disappeared into the back room to return, shortly, with several legal-size envelopes and one large manila. He handed them all over, and Roger handed back cash peeled from the roll of bills he slipped from his pants pocket.

Roger left the shoe shop, dropping his mail on the passenger seat of his car. He hadn't stuck around to make small talk. Snyder wasn't interested in getting to know his customers; the less he knew about them, the way he had it figured, and rightly so, the better off he was. All he cared about was the income they brought him, and how he, personally, could continue making damned sure there was never a hint, or rumor, that he didn't perform his services, as advertised, with the utmost discretion and expertise. It was a good indication of his trustworthiness that he was still alive and kicking; not a breath of derogatory comment hinted as to him being anything but fully adept at his job. In a business where clients were always paranoid, his record in providing his services for them was rock solid.

Roger didn't bother reading his mail, even after he arrived at the new apartment he'd leased under an alias. Totally involved in his quest to find Terrence's killer, or killers, hopefully determining the why behind Terrence being killed, he thought it ludicrous to sort through any new business proposals, especially since, if and when this was finished, he'd likely return to Seattle to try and find out why Evan was murdered.

It was a chance glance at the manila envelope's Seattle postmark, not rabid curiosity as regarded its contents, which had him, drink in hand, reach for and open it. If he, likewise, subconsciously recognized the outside handwriting as that of

Evan, it didn't register because of how long it had been since he'd received any incoming correspondence from the dead man by way of comparison.

Certainly, he didn't expect what he found inside the file folder that Evan had mailed him. He was so disinclined to believe it, as a matter of fact, that he immediately went to the secret hiding place he'd provided for the file folder given him to identify Bruce Franklin for termination, as well as for the folder that had once belonged to Terrence and identified Howard Cahn for termination; the latter passed to him via Brad.

He looked at the pictures of all three victims, having lined them up, one beside the other: Howard Cahn, Bruce Franklin, and the man called Lenox Pratt. All three looked exactly alike: chubby faces, gray hair, 5'10", blue eyes, and same age. If Bruce Franklin and Lenox Pratt wore glasses, where Howard Cahn did not…if Cahn and Franklin had a mustaches, Pratt clean-shaven …if Pratt had slightly longer hair than the other two…there was still no denying they could have been one and the same.

Roger sat back, glancing at the facades of all three files and noticed the similarity of arrangements and bindings that told him they'd all been compiled by the same source.

For some reason, contracts had successfully been put out on three men who looked so much alike that they could have been triplets. For some reason, the issuer, or issuers, of those contracts was likely responsible for the death of one of Roger's friends, maybe, even, the death of the missing second. For some reason, a contract had, likewise, been put out on Roger.

He still didn't know what in the hell was going down, but he did have every intention of finding out, and soon. If, as Sally Taln had been coaxed into confessing before dying, Lena Queenlin had answers, Roger was more determined than ever to have at them.

CHAPTER TWENTY-THREE

IT WAS MORE THAN a little ironic that Lena Queenlin was marked for death for information acquired by her only *after* Sally Taln implicated her to Roger as a source for the answers he was after. It was additionally ironic that she acquired it only just a short time before Roger arrived to coax it from her. Finally, it was ironic that her obtaining the information had resulted from Roger's rumored appearance in Seattle, and by his nosing around in regard to Evan Callen's murder, which had sent Gerold Lindsey into extreme paranoia and renewed impotency. Gerold thought to relieve his latest inner turmoil, and conquer his latest sexual impasse, by getting his troubles off his chest to Lena, rationalizing that her crypto-top-secret clearance was due to come through at any moment; that she didn't already have it was, by then, in his opinion, merely a formality.

"You have to accept the social climate at that time," he told her. "I mean, it was utter turmoil. Hitler, on the march, had already claimed a good part of Europe. The few countries not yet feeling the stomp of Nazi jackboots were seriously anticipating the day they *would*. Then, amid all of the rumors of Hitler's scientists working on the development of heavy water for nuclear reactions, and on rocket mechanics for perfecting V-5 capabilities, there began the rumors of his genetic experiments. If it was a natural response for those in the free world, at the time, to rush into more extensive nuclear and rocket research to combat the threat of his advancements, the same held true of the experiments he was apparently conducting…." He paused.

"…with and on people."

"With and on people?" Lena tried to keep her tone merely interested, rather than hint, even vaguely, of condemnation. Now that she had finally brought Gerold to the point of no return, she didn't want him to stop just because she gave the impression that she was disgusted by whatever he told her.

"Hitler's people were doing research on twins, triplets, quadruplets, and on just such single-cell divisions, on up the line," Gerold continued. It had taken him so long to decide to get it all out that Lena would really have been hard pressed to stop him, now, even if she'd wanted. "Several papers, regarding specific Nazi research in this field, were smuggled out of Germany and brought to the attention of the U.S. scientific community. The research involved aspects of certain experiments being conducted as regarded telepathic communication, the transmission of thoughts, over great distances, without the complications afforded by radio or other mechanical transmission devices. As you can well imagine, the very idea of Hitler suddenly having at his disposal a means of communication above and beyond that required by radio frequencies was enough to get more than a few of our side upset. It would have meant no chance of our interrupting any such communications, or of even knowing when and if they occurred. A German spy planted in some key position would need do nothing more than look at a secret document in order to transmit it, on the spot, to a twin or triplicate recipient in Germany, thousands of miles away, who could put it directly to paper."

"Good God!" Lena said into the sudden pause, offering that as her encouragement for him to proceed. She didn't yet see where any such research by Hitler, or by the Allies, could in anyway affect the here and now, especially bring on Gerold's bouts of paranoia and impotency. Had anything become of such research, it would have leaked long before now. When, in fact, such things as telepathic communication were still considered merely slights-of-hand performed by magicians and so-called mind readers in the prestidigitation business. While some colleges, universities, and research facilities were finally beginning, or so it seemed, to take a renewed interest in arcane subjects like ESP, there had never, past or present, been any major breakthroughs in that field, at least as far as Lena knew.

"It was only natural defensive positioning, on our side, that necessitated our instigating such projects on our own, in order to counter any possibilities of enemy advancements," Gerold continued. "Our research in mind communication was Code Name ABABA and was located at a facility in Aberlene, Pennsylvania."

"ABABA," Lena echoed, merely in indication that she paid attention and continued to offer a willing ear.

"Since all reports indicated that Hitler's research centered primarily on multiple-birth siblings from one multiple-divided single egg, supposedly having determined, by the time we received our copies of the files, that those defined the group most inclined toward success, ABABA immediately began its concentrated research along similar lines. Before the project was dissolved, many years after the war, due to inconclusive results, it had dealt with countless twins, triplets, quadruplets, et al; all acquired through state- or federally-financed and operated orphanages and adoptive institutions."

He drifted into another pause that Lena needlessly feared was him having second thoughts about saying what he was saying.

"How could all of that, having happened so many years ago, come back to haunt you, now?" she asked, determined to hear it all.

"ABABA was initiated under the auspices of our particular intelligence organization," Gerold said. "In effect, the responsibility for it still lies with us, AKA with me, with you, to this very day."

"But, there is no more ABABA, is there? Didn't you just say it was dissolved?

"Oh, it was, for all intents and purposes, dissolved, all right," Gerold verified, "after having been carried out for far longer than it ever should have been. All remaining experimental subjects, at conclusion, were separated from their siblings, and from other test subjects, to prevent future communication and note-comparing, given intensive psychological debriefings to relieve them of any memories, and farmed out to various parts of the country to begin 'normal' lives. Certainly, we don't want it to come out, now, even all of these years later, that our side, long after Hitler left the scene, was still involved in trying to see if his original research had merit."

"Of course, I see the reasoning behind that," Lena agreed. Definitely, she wanted Gerold to think she was sympathetic and on his side. "That still doesn't explain why there's any problem today. Unless...?"

"Unless what?" Gerold asked, curious to see how astute Lena might be with just the input he'd provided.

"Memories thought erased have returned?"

"Actually, more complex than that," Gerold said. With what he'd given her to work, her interpretation had logic. However, the reality offered far more serious repercussions than would the simple revelation, after all of these years, that the U.S. had been involved in telepathic communications research during World War II, and, for several years, thereafter.

There was another lengthy pause, once again interrupted by Lena. "How much more complex?" she asked, impatient, although she tried not to sound that way.

"At one point during research, ABABA subjects under-went experimentation with a heavy-metal drug, *di-siphol-tri-hydroxene-II*," Gerold said. "Without boring you with a detailed scientific molecular analysis, of which not even I'm sure, suffice it to say that when introduced into the human system, it appar-ently has a decidedly bad tendency to stick around indefinitely, within certain body tissues, including those of the brain. The assumption, of course, based upon animal testing, was that administering the drug was worth the risk, in that it could heighten certain psychic capabilities otherwise dormant, as well as enhance those already in evidence. In fact, initial results proved so successful as to encourage continued use even after patients began complaining of adverse reactions."

"Adverse reactions, consisting of…?" Lena asked.

"Mainly spontaneous convulsions," Gerold said. "Think epileptic fits. Then, there was a death. Even one death is reason to keep ABABA under wraps, even after the project is long dissolved. There are always plenty of people ready to be enraged by such things as human experimentation without even bringing death into the equation."

"I see," Lena agreed.

"I doubt it!" Gerold begged to differ. He wanted to impress upon her the full impact of what had raised such havoc with his nervous system over these past few weeks. "What you see is only the tip of the iceberg."

If there was more Gerold needed to say, possibly to link previously dropped references to a missing letter in a Seattle mailbox, and a body somehow missing….

"Experimentation with the drug stopped," Gerold continued, "without more deaths…until, that is, just a few weeks ago when one of the few remaining test subjects went into massive convulsions and died in a Washington State fishing stream."

"So many years after the fact?" Simultaneously, Lena knew it often took years to determine health damage done by exposure to such things as radiation or pollutants.

"So, it would seem," Gerold verified. "Our experts, with far more sophisticated scientific methodology available to them, today, than when the project was officially wrapped, pinpointed the problem as *di-siphol-tri-hydroxene-II*," and correctly predicted the other still-living ABABA subjects would experience similar deaths. So, our original plan was to round them all up, sequester them in crypto-top secret sites known to only a select few on a need-to-know basis, and let them live out their last days. Even the chance of one of them dropping dead on a city street and being taken to a local hospital, with a resulting correct diagnosis of death-by-heavy-metal diagnosis, would result in all sorts of repercussions leading troublemakers directly to our doorstep. *Di-siphol-tri-hydroxene-II* is still on every restricted-drug-access list, and any recognizably high concentrations of it within any human body, dead or alive, will raise all sorts of red flags."

"No wonder you're under such pressure!" Lena sympathized and wondered what Zregory Litzen would make of this startling information. Blackmail?

"Major problems, of course—quite aside from subjects by now so 'into' their present life-styles that they weren't too pleased to be herded off, yet again, only this time to die. Not to mention how our monitoring of subjects, over the years, had grown so unacceptably lax that at least one of the group had fallen off the grid completely and had to be tracked down."

"Murder isn't drawing unwanted attention?"

"Murder by bullet provides a viable reason for death, no need to delve any farther. *Di-siphol-tri-hydroxene-II* isn't something that turns up in any typical drug test. However, have one or more people die of convulsions, no immediate explanation seen to exist, and see where that goes. Therefore, independent agents were hired for hits, given anything but the real reasons for the terminations. In turn, the terminating agents were designated for erasure, in order to murky any trails that might lead back to us."

"Jesus!" Lena said, rolling beside him on the bed into a position that put her head on his naked chest. She could hear the loudness of his heart as it beat at far more than its normal tempo. "No wonder you're in such a state."

"They're all dead, now, though, but one," Gerold said. "An independent agent, Roger Lenic. He should be dead, too, except he somehow escaped to resurface, recently, we think, in Seattle, where he's been probing into the death of another independent agent we used in an ABABA termination. Lenic is a loose canon we can't seem to get under control."

"You will," Lena assured. "I'm sure it's only a matter of time."

She had all of the answers she needed, except for one.

"What about that missing letter in the Seattle mail?" she

asked, surprised by how quickly Gerold grabbed a handful of her hair and pulled her head up to face him.

"How do you know about the letter?" he asked loudly, his eyes bugging with suspicion.

"*You* told me," she reminded, fearful that she wasn't going to live to pass on any of this to Zregory. It would be ever so ironic if she were killed, now, because of something Gerold had told her before and simply forgotten having told her. "Remember?" she pleaded and overlooked the pain of his fingers in her hair. "*You* mentioned it the other evening," she persisted, hoping to God he wasn't suddenly as senile as he was impotent. "You told me some agent, who should have been terminated, was still missing; another, before dying, had somehow slipped some kind of letter, or package, into the Seattle mail system."

"Yes, I guess I do remember saying something to that effect," he admitted in a moment of sudden lucidity. He returned her head to his chest, releasing his finger-hold on her hair. "Yes, of course, I remember. I'm sorry."

Lena felt a definite flood of relief. She trailed her right hand down his stomach to his groin. She fondled his limp penis.

"It was good to talk about it, wasn't it?" she said, still not completely over her scare. "It's always better to talk it over and get it out in the open, with someone you can trust, so it's not quite as bad as when entirely cooped up inside of you. I'm right, aren't I? Or am I mistaken in how our little talk has just cured of your latest bout of soft dick?"

"You're right, of course," he said, pushing her face down to his lap to service him. "Oh, Jesus, my wonderful, wonderful Lena, you are always so, so right about everything."

CHAPTER TWENTY-FOUR

ROGER KILLED HER, because it was expedient for him to do so. If Lena Queenlin could be persuaded to spill her guts to him, and she had been, she couldn't be expected to keep silent when her own side asked her to supply them with a description of Roger. Her boss, Gerold Lindsey, probably already had enough on the missing independent agent, Roger Lenic, on file, to put two and two together and get four. Roger preferred Lindsey be kept guessing for as long as possible, though, especially since that man was now on the tiptop of Roger's shit-list.

If Roger was right in his assumption that both of his friends, Evan and Terrence, had been contracted by George Lindsey, or by Lindsey's representatives, on behalf of Lindsey's top-secret intelligence agency, to kill subjects of the ABABA project, and, then, been eliminated by Lindsey's men to cover Lindsey's and Lindsey's intelligence-agency's asses, then Lindsey was about to become another victim. The pieces certainly all seemed in place now that Lena had conveniently spilled her guts, in more ways than one. Howard Cahn, Lenox Pratt, killed respectively by Terrence Flag and Evan Callan, were two of the triplets that included Bruce Franklin, the latter the man Roger was hired to terminate.

"You're right," came the voice of Gerold Lindsey over the speaker of the tape recorder found in Lena Queenllin's bed. "Oh, Jesus, my wonderful, wonderful Lena, you are so right!"

Roger switched off the play and pressed the eject button. He had already heard the tape through once, and he had no desire to sit though all of its sexual grunts and groans again. Whatever conversation that followed the rutting wasn't nearly as interesting as the conversation before it, anyway.

Having retrieved the tape cartridge from Lena's hidden tape recorder, Roger now turned the incriminating evidence in his large fingers and wondered, suddenly, why Lena had such a tape to begin with. Probably, he should have made it a point to find out, except that, once having gotten all of the information he really thought he'd needed from her, he'd gotten rid of her. It was only in retrospect, the tape found, that he began to see just how stupid she was to have had such a piece of incriminating evidence around for anyone, including him, to find, and he began to wonder if Gerold Lindsey could possibly know that his conversations in that bedroom had been recorded. More likely, Lena had been out to formulate her insurance policy to stand her in good stead if and when Lindsey got tired of her.

"Valuable! Valuable!" Roger said; his eyes were still on the cassette in hand. He now possessed the firing cap that could blow this whole nasty stick of ABABA dynamite up in Gerold Lindsey's face. The bastard had worried about Roger turning up something and had inadvertently obliged by providing it.

He laid the cassette to one side and opened the top drawer of the desk at which he was seated. He pulled out a sheet of stationery, an envelope, and a roll of stamps.

Brad—

Hold this for a week. If I don't come by for it by then, I probably won't be coming by, period; so, then feel free to hand this over to the police, to the newspapers, or to whomever else you think might provide you the most satisfaction. The man's voice on the tape is Gerold Lindsey, with U.S. intelligence. The woman's voice is his fellow intelligence agent and one-time mistress, Lena Queenlin, now deceased.

—Ciao! Roger.

He wrapped the letter around the tape and attached the two with a rubber band. After addressing the envelope and putting the wrapped cassette inside, he added more than enough stamps to the outside to see the package successfully through the mail.

He went to the door that connected the apartment to the hallway, and he checked through the fish-eye peephole, seeing no one outside. He slipped out of the apartment, going as far as the mail-drop between the elevators. He slid the letter, with its incriminating evidence, into the slot, and watched it drop toward the secured pick-up box in the basement.

He went back to Lena's apartment, having mailed the evidence as a simple precaution. Although he had been successful enough getting this far, he couldn't be completely sure he was going to get any farther. If he didn't make it, he wanted the noose still placed around Gerold Lindsey's damned neck in order to, even if from the grave, blacken the reputation of that man and his agency. If Roger didn't make it, he felt confident Brad would know what to do. After all, Brad had already proven competent and certainly had the money necessary to pick up on Roger's failure, should there be one

He decided to give the place one more thorough go-through, just in case there was something else, yet missed, that Lena might have carelessly left lying around.

CHAPTER TWENTY-FIVE

"KILL HER!" Edgar Winter said over the telephone and, then, replaced the receiver on its hook. He turned to Gerold Lindsey who sat across from him.

Gerold looked and was very nervous; he had every right to be. All of his last few weeks of hard work and planning had about blown up in his face, not because of the machinations of Roger Lenic but because Gerold had suddenly become linked to a likely high-level security leak.

"I'll owe you one after this, Edgar," Gerold said, using his handkerchief to wipe sweat from his furrowed brow.

"What are friends for, right?" Edgar asked. Damned right, Gerold would owe him big time! Something like this could mean Gerold Lindsey's bloody head, and Edgar knew it. That's why Edgar brought the problem to Gerold, it being Gerold's problem, it being Edgar's purpose to build up favors. Edgar didn't have any proof-positive, yet, that Gerold had passed state secrets to Lena Queenlin, but he, and anyone else, could pretty well assume that from what evidence Edgar did have, especially now with Gerold so damned anxious to have the woman blown away, Edgar having presented him with the circumstantial evidence to indicate Lena was an enemy mole.

Why else would she have turned up at the house of none other than Zregory Litzen who, though never convicted of anything, could definitely raise suspicions, especially with any meeting with Lena. Gerold, even more than Edgar, obviously knowing that.

Edgar and Gerold sat back and waited, Gerold thanking the good luck that had provided Edgar the good sense to come to Gerold with this. How ironic that it had been Gerold's instigation of proceedings to upgrade Lena's security clearance that had put Edgar on her tail in the first place. If Edgar hadn't been shadowing her, as one standard routine for Lena's upgrade to a crypto-top-secret status, the woman might have proceeded on her merry way to gum up the works—if she hadn't gummed them up already.

It seemed forever before the phone finally rang, Edgar saying the few terse words that left Gerold more nervous.

"Trouble." Gerold said; it wasn't so much a question as it was a statement.

"I think maybe you'd better come along with me on this," Edgar said, getting to his feet. "We're liable to have to call in some of your other friends to keep this on the hush-hush, in that it seems someone beat us to the punch, as far as elimination of your girlfriend. My men interrupted the killer while he was still ransacking her apartment. Two of my men are dead. The guy in question is wounded and pinned down. There's a helluva lot of noise being made, which means cops to be reckoned with."

It wasn't the police, though, that had Gerold worried. In fact, the police were the least of his worries. In any operation involving the police and any U.S. intelligence agency, the later always took precedence, especially when citing "national security."

CHAPTER TWENTY-SIX

YES, VIRGINIA, MAYBE THERE really *is* a Santa Claus, Gerold thought as he weaved his car through the maze of heavy traffic. Although he was reluctant to believe himself finally gifted with the ABABA problems finally swept completely under the rug, he had reached the point where he breathed easier. Six months without repercussions seemed time enough for anything bad to happen that was going to happen.

My God, he had been fortunate! Not only had Lena evidently not had time to pass on her information, but the raid on her apartment had netted and eliminated Roger Lenic in the bargain. Therefore, all of the ABABA loose strings had been gathered up and neatly tied, except for whatever Evan Callen had posted, and to whom, from that Seattle post office just prior to his termination. Even that, however, as time passed, seemed of less and less significance. Hell, it could, by now, logically be assumed that he'd merely mailed some piece of personal correspondence, nothing to do with anything to implicate Gerold or the U.S. in any secret project, resulting murders, and covers-up.

Of course, Gerold came out of it owing Edgar Winter. Considering everything, though, that was a small enough concession. In fact, he could probably get out of even that obligation by pointing out how Edgar, himself, had become so involved as soon as he came to Gerold about Lena, instead of reporting Gerold's involvement with the woman through proper channels. In the end, though, there was little for Gerold to gain by alienating an obvious ally, especially since Gerold, by making those few phone calls which brought Edgar his promotion, tied the man even tighter to Gerold's apron strings. God only knew when Gerold might, once again, find it advantageous to access Edgar's good will and willingness to serve.

So, hallelujah, there was still the chance of miracles in this modern day and age, not the least being how Gerold had already found someone to substitute for Lena's love-making. Lovely, lovely, Kandra Kareen, with her honey-colored hair, blue eyes, and breasts like overripe melons. Just thinking of her gave him the hard-on he'd soon be plowing away inside her.

Definitely, he had learned his lesson by the scare he'd had from his relationship with Lena. No way, ever again, would he get diarrhea of the mouth with *any* woman. His relationship with Kandra, and any woman, thereafter, would be purely on a sexual basis. Considering just how good Kandra was in the sack, that fit his plans quite nicely—yes, please, and thank you very much!

CHAPTER TWENTY-SEVEN

BRAD NELSON LAY BELLY-DOWN on the rooftop and watched the car that pulled to the curb and stopped in front of the building just down and across from him.

He worked the butt of his rifle more comfortably into his right shoulder for additional support and lined up Gerold Lindsey in the rifle's powerful sights.

As Gerold walked to the front door of the apartment building, Brad took a short in-draw of breath, held it, and squeezed the trigger.

Gerold dropped to the pavement, dead on arrival. The exhilarating shudder of sweet revenge that Brad felt for the death of his lover, Terrence Flag, came very close to orgasmic.

ABOUT THE AUTHOR

WILLIAM MALTESE, the internationally bestselling author of novels, short story collections, and his popular Stud Draqual Mystery Series, has published (under various pseudonyms) close to two hundred books in genres including gay and straight erotica, sci-fi, science-fantasy, mystery, romance, western, adventure, espionage, cooking, wine, and children. With a Business/Advertising degree, Maltese enlisted in the U.S. Army, where he achieved and was honorably discharged at a Sergeant (E-5) rank. Presently, he divides his time between the Pacific Northwest and New York City. You can visit his websites or email him at:

www.williammaltese.com
www.myspace.com/williammaltese
www.facebook.com/williammaltese

email: williammaltese@yahoo.com

www.ingramcontent.com/pod-product-compliance
Lightning Source LLC
Chambersburg PA
CBHW050407260626
47156CB00003B/912

WELCOME TO THE GREY ZONE...

...And its nefarious and shadowy landscape that knows no international borders.

....Whose each and every individual has special expertise, but no permanent ties or allegiances to any nationalities, countries, or governments. If you want a landmark statue shattered in New York City, a bridge blown in London, a tower toppled in Paris—but don't want any evidence left around to tie you to the crimes— you'll find people in the GREY ZONE who'll sign on to accomplish any and all of that—for a price!

Freelance special agents Troy Candle, Gregory Ohm, Johan Darnel, David Rheingold, and Ken Mal are among those in the GREY ZONE who are about to be—or already have been—recently hired...to bury the *INCIDENT AT BRIMZINSKY*!

Borgo Press Books by WILLIAM MALTESE

INCIDENT AT BRIMZINSKY

SPIES AND LIES, BOOK TWO

WILLIAM MALTESE

THE BORGO PRESS
MMXI

INCIDENT AT BRIMZINSKY

FIRST EDITION

Published by Wildside Press LLC

www.wildsidebooks.com

DEDICATION

To Michael Burgess, Editor,

and John Betancourt, Publisher,

Without whose double-vision there would be none of these Wildside/Borgo doubled-novel books.

CONTENTS

CHAPTER ONE

THE DARKNESS WAS complete except for the whites of the rolled-back starring eyes of the dead man at the bottom of the trench in Egypt's Tomb 42 atop the escarpment at Egypt's Aswan.

The dead man was Troy Candle, or, anyway, that's what official reports said when written up, filed away, and forgotten, as was the paperwork of most unsolved crimes that cluttered the backroom shelves at Aswan police headquarters; although, at the time, a lot of people scratched their heads and wondered why Candle was in Egypt, in general, and in that hole, in particular. He was a member of a rather nefarious group of freelance intelligence agents, known to exist within the murky Grey Zone, and he had last been heard from while selling blueprints of a Soviet naval installation to Red Chinese contacts in Berchtesgaden. Before that, he had been somehow involved in the transfer of a reputed large cache of WWII Nazi gold from its supposedly long-lasting hiding place in a communist country to the vaults of a prominent Swiss bank. Neither of which occurred anywhere in, nor near, Egypt. Besides which, there was no evidence of his having entered the country through legal channels, certainly no passport, or other travel papers, forged or otherwise, found on his person. The movements of all other foreigners in Aswan (ten of them at the Hotel Oberoi, six at the New Cataracts) were monitored closely by local authorities, for some kind of connect with Candle, but nothing suspicious turned up; although, Jergen Deetzhin, as a citizen of East Germany, drew temporary suspi-

cion because of Candle's previously suspected involvement in the transfer of the old German (Nazi) gold.

One by one, however, the businessmen, Deetzhin included, turned out pretty much who they purported to be. Granted, Denny Slizer was involved in a shady monetary deal that concerned the shipment of foreign currencies gathered on the country's black market, but he, or that, apparently had nothing to do with Candle. Verification of which could have been privately attested to by any one of the several top-ranking Egyptian police and government officials who received large cuts off the top of Slizer's profits.

In truth, not even Gregory Ohm, the man whose hands pulled the piano wire through Candle's windpipe, like a warm knife slicing butter, had any real knowledge as to why his victim was ordered terminated.

The Egyptian authorities could have looked far and wide for any reference to Ohm in their records of foreigners in Egypt, the week of Candle's death, and found no record of him, either. Ohm hadn't arrived via Cairo or Alexandria. Nor had he entered from the south, via Khartoum. He'd come from the west, across the Libyan border, entering Egypt by camel. He'd crossed vast tracts of desert wasteland which were just as wild and rugged as they'd been when caravans of old had more regularly tracked through the same wilderness. Since he had, at one time, been assigned to Egypt, back when his nationality was more clearly defined, his loyalties more centralized (rather than given to the highest bidder), he'd traveled with neither friend nor guide. The two Arabs he had chanced to meet along the way, this last visit, showed no recognition of him being anyone but the fellow nomad he purported to be (his mastery of the language and of the customs nearly perfect), and the duo would have passed him on by, without too much thought, except Ohm hadn't lived as long as he had without covering every contingency. If he left the Arabs and their camels dead in the desert, soon buried in shifting sand atop the piled stones and shallow graves he'd

initially provided, he had no qualms about what he'd done. It was merely the "fate" of those Arabs to have had their luck run out in the sandy wastes of the deep Sahara.

The meeting between Ohm and Candle had been planned not by Ohm but by the people who hired him. This hadn't been one of those assignments where he was left to his own wiles as to how to carry it out. This one was a piece of cake, handed him on a silver platter, wrapped up for him in prior blue ribbons, detailed right to the point where the wire sliced deep and splashed Candle's blood and phlegm over Ohm's shirt sleeves, not to mention over just about everything else.

According to the kill-plan, Candle had been told that Ohm had something in his possession which Candle had obviously wanted enough to come to Tomb 42 to buy. What that was, exactly, Ohm never did find out, although he later wished that he had held off the termination for at least as long as it would have taken him to find out. But, everything had worked so like clockwork, at the time, he'd been swept along in the euphoria of participating in something so obviously choreographed to perfection. It was so seldom a plan—any plan—played through without some kind of botch-up, that Ohm had simply been caught up in the sheer magic of the moment. Besides, it was never wise policy to question too closely the whys behind any operation. Employers weren't inclined to use too inquisitive employees a second time, if even finishing to use them a first time. The chances of an agent staying alive were usually in direct proportion to the amount of information he *didn't* possess regarding motives behind any operation. Of course, there was a certain amount of knowledge allowed without retribution. Agents, good ones, were too hard to come by, within the ranks of freelance Grey-Zoners available at any one time, to bump them off indiscriminately. Seldom were vacancies filled with the speed of depletions. Those who operated as Grey-Zone free-lancers provided services which, sooner or later, were needed, by whatever official side.

It was the fact that the termination of Candle, such a well-

known Grey-area agent, was carried out by Ohm, another well-known Grey-Zone agent, that eventually did raise Ohm's curiosity about the kill. But, by the time he got around to asking questions, reflective, indiscreet ones, in the bar of the Britannia Hotel in London, it was a mite too late.

CHAPTER TWO

JOHAN DARNEL EXITED the Paris to Amsterdam train at Gate 6 and took the stairway down the labyrinth of the main terminal building. He wasn't encumbered by any bags, because he hadn't brought any with him. He didn't need any. Not for a quick night on the town. He was scheduled out the next morning at five. That gave him plenty of time.

Taxis were lined up outside, but Johan didn't need a taxi. He wasn't going that far.

He took the access to the mainland, leaving the Central Railroad Station which had been constructed (Johan couldn't remember when), on a few thousand (he couldn't remember the exact number) piles sunk to extend a small natural island in the harbor. He hit Damrak Street, skirting the small basin that acted as docking area for local boats leaving every half an hour, during the day, for tours of the city canals, but which was, now, empty, and dark. Johan's light-weight London Fog coat was more than adequate protection against the slight breeze.

He turned off Damrak, knowing he was in familiar territory even before the first red light caught his eye up ahead. He could think of nowhere that the term "red-light district" was more apropos than in Amsterdam.

Another turn brought him into a small alley, the gauntlet-like buildings with windows that looked out on the small pathway running between. The windows had curtains, most of which were thrown open to reveal a maximum of two rooms behind glass. The space just beyond usually contained but one small

chair. The other room was usually a little larger, with a bed or, maybe, with only a mattress on its floor.

Ladies of the evening sat in the chairs, freely plying their wares without leaving the relative comfort of their little cubby-holes. In one form of undress or another, they smiled at potential customers, licked lips coquettishly or lasciviously, and beckoned passersby in close enough to lip-read how much it cost to join the ladies on the other side of the glass and closed doors.

Johan didn't stop. Not on that particular street anyway. Neither did he snicker nor, otherwise, act embarrassed, like one group of young men who were obviously tourists there for the first time.

A few streets away, along one of the city's hundred canals, were late-night establishments with displayed pictures on the sidewalk, and neon signs on facades, that announced live sex shows ("Thirty-six different positions!" one barker cried), porno movies, and girlie shows.

Interspersed, here and there, among everything else, were dirty-book stores and the "sex-toy" shops selling everything from edible black-lace panties to massive latex dildos.

The red-light district maze appeared complicated to the uninitiated. Tourists, who hadn't bothered acquainting themselves with the often confusing grid system of canals and winding streets, were often lost. The only direction offered by the ladies in the windows had nothing whatsoever to do with how one located the Hotel American.

Johan had been the route often enough so its labyrinth was familiar. He had long ago become jaded enough to the novelties offered by the shops and by the entertainment centers not to be tempted to move in close for even a peek at the latest video or live show of "Big Black" Jack taking on the whole Sultan's harem. So, when he stopped, momentarily, it wasn't to do any prurient sight-seeing, merely to massage a recently recurring pain, likely muscle-strain, in his right arm.

When he reached his final destination, its red curtain was closed, but there was light seeping out around the cracks. Johan

wasn't put off by all signs of the cubbyhole's occupant being presently busy. He'd called ahead, never willing to take the chance of not having Heidi Tenkaarn available when he wanted.

He knocked on the door that bordered her window. The door, mainly glass, was curtained with the same red material that draped the window. The red of the door slid to one side, showing a brief glimpse of a pretty face before the door came open.

"Long time, no see, handsome!" Heidi said, sidestepping to let Johan on in. Immediately, she closed the door behind them and leaned back against it to face the man now inside.

Heidi was a statuesque brunette whose healthy mane of naturally raven hair was supplemented by several expensive "falls" and extensions that confused where real hair left off and false began. She had an attractive face that had obviously been even more attractive when she was younger. Her makeup consisted of something that gave her an attractive, although decidedly artificial, tan. After all, she worked nights and spent most of her days sleeping in preparation for her evenings. Her lips were painted a bright, wet red. Her eyelids had just the faintest shadowing of light violet.

Her breasts were large and firm, lifted by a brassiere with half-cups that threatened spilling their contents over its black leather. The brassiere cups were notched so her hard nipples were not only visible but poked on through.

She wore leather pants, notched at the crotch to reveal her entire pubic area. The pants fit like second skin; her boots (spike-heeled and patent leather), climbed high up her shapely legs to her thighs.

On the whole, within the dim lighting, Heidi looked exceptionally good. If Johan might have found someone a little better looking, someone a good deal younger, by merely taking a bit more time to cruise the streets, he wasn't out for youth, or for beauty. He was out for the no-nonsense expertise Heidi offered that very few women in Amsterdam did (and Johan knew this from experience).

"Let's not waste any time, shall we?" Johan said, turning to

enter the back room. He knew the way.

He began to undress, hearing the definite re-locking of the outside door just before Heidi came to join him. The woman leaned against one wall, her arms folded across her ample breasts. She eyed his nakedness emerging from his discarded clothing and was impressed as always; this said a good deal about the way Johan kept care of himself. After all, Heidi had seen a good deal of naked men in her time with whom to make comparisons. Johan, although a good deal older than some of those Heidi took on, still managed a tightness of physique which other younger men had long since surrendered to pot bellies and fallen butts.

Heidi had more than once wondered about Johan's job, originally having suspected something to do with construction until realizing he didn't have nearly enough calluses. Heidi, of course never went so far as to ask. She had learned a long time ago that her customers would volunteer whatever information they thought she should have. Since Johan never volunteered anything, he clearly insinuated it was none of her business. So be it!

When Johan was finally stripped naked and stood, facing Heidi, he was in a full state of penile erection. He followed Heidi to the center of the back room. He raised both arms toward the ceiling, allowing Heidi to affix his wrists to manacles suspended from two free-hanging chains whose other ends were bolted securely to the ceiling.

"Well, now, Slave," Heidi said, gliding the tips of her red-lacquered nails down Johan's naked back, pulling her hand away long enough to deliver a hearty whack to his ass that sounded very much like a rifle shot fired within a very close space. Johan groaned obvious pleasure. "Wait until you see what your Momma has planned for you this evening."

She went to one of three bureaus along one wall. She opened the top drawer, selecting a cat-o'-nine tails from the assortment of bondage-and-discipline accoutrements now at her disposal.

She turned her attention back to Johan and walked up close

to his hanging body to run the butt end of her whip down the total length of his muscled back and into the crack of his firmly muscled butt. The sensation of which he was most aware, at the moment, though, was the return of pain to his right arm which he hoped to hell wasn't going, in any way, shape, or form, to interfere with this long-anticipated evening of fun and games with Heidi.

CHAPTER THREE

THERE WAS NO DENYING that Rome's Coliseum looked beautiful by moonlight. This might have had something to do with why the place where Denver Rheingold now stood was called Luna Park. But, Denver wasn't there for the view—at least not the one afforded by the floodlights which turned the prominent ruin bright within the darkness.

There was a time, not so many years ago, when Denver would have found himself over at the Coliseum at this time of the night, wandering through its outer galleries. That action, however, had since moved across the street to the park, driven there by heavy tourist traffic during the day (and other, more clandestine, foot traffic at night) over the preceding years, which had put antiquity authorities to seriously wondering about the likely detrimental extent of 24/7 wear and tear on the old structure. As a result, the Coliseum was, now, nightly blocked off, after official closing.

Denver turned from the balustrade that he leaned on, putting his back toward the Coliseum and the equally well-known Arch of Constantine. To his right was the Palatine beyond the Via de St. Gregorio. To his left was the Via Claudia that bordered the park's eastern edge. In front of him was a darkness filled with people in movement as they walked along gravel pathways, around ruins, and through shrubbery that, in the darkness, offered niches for privacy.

Denver had never really been quite certain what exactly these particular immediate "park" ruins represented. Someone had

once said they were part of the Baths of Caracalla. But, Denver had since discovered that the Baths were farther south, across the Viale delle Terme. Most likely, then, what he saw, now, was some part of the ruined Villa Celimontana; although, in the end, he supposed it really didn't make all that much difference. Denver was no more there as a buff of archaeology than he was there to see the Coliseum by moonlight.

He entered the deeper darkness, allowing himself to become a part of it, removing himself completely from any spillover of light that managed to span the distance from the amphitheater. He began paying particular attention to those shadows moving with him, knowing that they had been brought to this place, this night, for the same reason he was there.

It was still early. Denver could tell that without even checking his wristwatch, because there would be no military personnel after nine 'clock, all of them hurrying back to their barracks to meet evening curfews. One young soldier, his silhouette the same classical features that turned Denver on to Greco-Roman art so many years before, lit a cigarette that illuminated his handsome face.

Denver was tempted, but he decided not to take advantage of the obvious invitation to make an approach. The military studs were out to earn a little extra cash. Not that Denver had anything against paying. As a matter of fact, trying to find an Italian, in the military or not, who didn't charge, was like finding a needle in a haystack. As much as the Italian male often turned out to be the hottest and most sexually willing, there was something about his character which demanded monetary rationalization for whatever his performance. Denver figured, therefore, since he likely would be paying sometime during the course of the evening, there was no need for him to jump at the first piece of offered-up merchandise that chanced crossing his pathway. Italy, in general, Rome in particular, was full of attractive young men to be shopped and bought.

He moved deeper into the darkness, veering along a line of broken pillars whose upper portions had long since become

lost. The gravel of the pathway crunched against the soles of his shoes. He unfastened a couple more buttons of his shirt, it being one of those glorious summer evenings for which Rome is particularly noted. There was a slight breeze that saved the night from being too warm.

He stopped by one of the pillars, leaning against it. Once again, he found himself facing the Coliseum. Although this time, it was far enough away so that whatever light there was within its aura didn't reach as far as him.

Someone approached. Even in the darkness, Denver could tell that it was the same soldier from earlier, the lit cigarette still visible in the kid's cupped right hand.

"Nice night," the solider said in Italian. He dropped the cigarette to the ground and crushed it out in the gravel.

"I'm sorry, but I don't speak Italian," Denver said. "I'm American."

This was a lie on both counts. He was fluent in six languages, Italian one of them. He wasn't American but Argentinean, his grandparents having been Germans who, at the end of World War II, had taken advantage of Peron's largesse (and greediness for gold bullion), to find political asylum in South America.

"I speak a little English," the soldier said. "Enough, I think."

This turned out to be quite true. While his English was sometimes not the best, it was definitely enough to get across all that was needed, under the circumstances, beginning with the fact that his name was Giovani, ending with the fact that he had come out that evening to check on the action. What about Denver?

Denver shrugged and said something about the view. He wasn't quite yet convinced that the kid, out of all the others available that evening, was the one he wanted. There was someone else, strolling just out of clear eyesight, who Denver thought might be more interesting.

"Do you want to go to my friend's place for a drink?" Giovani asked, perhaps suspecting Denver's reluctance.

"I have to get back to my hotel," Denver lied once again,

compounding the lie by adding: "I have to fly to Firenze tomorrow."

Denver didn't want to go to anyone's place. If he did anything that evening, he wanted to do it right there. There was something about the combination of shadow and ruins, with Coliseum in the background, that gave this setting the right ambience Denver found ideal for good sex. The absence of bright lighting, and the shrubbery with available private niches within it, allowed him a sense of security and ease that he seldom found within the confines of any four walls.

"Oh," Giovani said. Obviously not discouraged, though, he added, "Then, step this way, just a bit."

Denver hesitated, trying one more time to discern the features of that other shadow that continued to prowl just beyond clear viewing.

"Come on," Giovani persisted.

Denver pushed himself away from the pillar and proceeded with apparent reluctance.

"I don't know," he said, knowing from past experience that the less anxious he appeared, at such moments, the more anxious Italian men seemed to become to have at him. "I think, maybe, I had just better go back to my hotel."

"Nah," Giovani said. They had stopped along the edge of one well-manicured hedge which meandered through the park. "Why return to your hotel?"

"It's getting late," Denver said. "I do have to fly to Firenze early tomorrow morning, and my wife…."

He left the lie about his wife hanging right where it was, as if it had just kind of slipped out, unaware, coaxed to light by some inherent guilt within him—guilt about his being where he was, with whom he was. The insinuation, of course, was planned. Denver knew that Italian men seemed always more turned on if they thought they were about to do it with a married man, instead of with just a common queer. The Italian male's sense of sexual perspective, as far as Denver was concerned, was always a bit hung up on macho image. That didn't, however, keep him

from using it to his advantage.

"Really, I do think I'd better go," he said, making a move that looked as if his sudden guilt had soured him on the whole scene. In reality, he wasn't going anywhere.

Giovani obviously had a lot of experience wooing paranoid tourists. Moving in on the apparently skittish Denver, Giovani's right hand brushed the man's crotch, and the young soldier whistled in appreciation that wasn't faked.

"Really, I think I'd better go," Denver repeated, simultaneously knowing he was definitely going to see this through to the end.

"Your wife is lucky," Giovani said. "She will be happy to see what you bring to your hotel bedroom. Yes?"

"My wife isn't feeling well this evening," Denver said.

"Mine, either," Giovani said.

"You're married, then?" Denver said and gave an audible sigh of relief that seemed to indicate he could feel much more at ease about all of this in the face of meeting a kindred spirit.

"Sure," Giovani said, as if he was surprised that Denver had assumed otherwise. "I have two children. And you?"

The kid looked hardly old enough to have even one child. Denver, though, didn't say that. They were probably both game-playing, after all. Game-playing was what this scene was all about. It was part of what got Denver high.

"Three children," Denver said, although he hadn't been in bed with a woman since Mary Perilli in high school. "Two boys; one girl."

"Very nice," Giovani said. Although, since his comment was accompanied by another brush of his hand across the bulge of Denver's crotch, it was a little hard to tell whether he had been referring to Denver's aroused condition, or to the virility of the man as a husband and father.

"My wife is having her period," Giovani said, moving in closer, as if inviting Denver to see for himself how the youth's ailing wife had left the kid in pretty much the same frustrated state of blue-balls that Denver was in.

Denver obliged by tentatively putting out his hand and then pulling it back, in seeming guilt, upon making contact.

"I really don't think I should be here," Denver said, well into his guilt routine by then. "Really, I just don't."

Come on, through here," Giovani said. He put his hand on Denver's arm and guided the man even deeper into the shrubbery. He faced Denver, there, amid the greenery, so close that the two couldn't help touching. "We don't really need our wives this evening, do we?"

Giovani was already unfastening the fly of Denver's trousers.

CHAPTER FOUR

TO SAY THAT KEN MAL and Gregory Ohm were friends
would be a definite misnomer. Few freelance agents within the
Grey Zone were friends, in that loyalties, in their line of business, changed with the mere passing of a few bits of currency
from one numbered Swiss bank account to another.

Therefore, it wasn't friendship that had Gregory give Ken
a call that night, against instructions which had specifically
stated that Gregory should remain incognito for at least three
months following the Troy Candle elimination in Aswan. What
prompted his call was his one flaw of character which possibly
doomed him to failure from the very moment he decided to
enter the spy business. Those who best survived those murky
waters the longest were the sharks that operated purely as loners
with an inherent "feel" for self-preservation.

In the pure sense of the word, Gregory wasn't a shark. Or,
if he was (his success in the business, after all, attributed to a
certain knack for his chosen field), he wasn't a Great White.
There were moments when he actually wished he was something other than what he had become. At those moments
(admittedly fewer and farther between as the years went by), he
mentally retraced (as well as he could), those steps which had
brought him from where he'd started out to where he'd ended
up. He tried to recall all of the crucial crossroads he'd encoun-
tered, along his way, and often conjectured as to how the ways
he'd chosen compared to other routes that might have been. He
had definite moments when he needed outside reinforcement to

assure him that he was right in doing all that he had done, and in doing what he was doing. Ken Mal could always be counted upon to provide just that.

Ken worked on assignment with Gregory only once; another reason Gregory saw him as ideal. There wasn't yet any malice or animosity between them, any long-festering grudges, or vendettas, any "points" yet made by one at the expense of the other. If they weren't friends, they weren't yet enemies, and they had at least one "thing" in common. That was Troy Candle. Not that Gregory or Ken ever worked *with* the man, but Candle had a reputation for having survived a long time in their business and in having made himself very rich in the process. All of which had Gregory now wondering, a little late in the day, what it was that Candle had finally done, who he had finally so deeply offended, that someone had arranged for his termination by Gregory?

Ken knew he was far better attuned to their profession than Gregory. That he agreed to come for drinks was the result of some responsive chord, deep inside of him, that reminded him of a time (long shoved into the background) when he had found himself in the same questioning state of mind that Gregory seemed to be in.

It was pure chance that Ken was available. While he'd been living in the Radcliffe Garden flat when he first met Gregory, the place had since become mainly just a mail drop, or, at the very most, a safe house for holding occasional people or documents in transit.

Having just wrapped an assignment in Lisbon, Ken had opted for his debriefing in London, and he'd been back in the flat for only a week when Gregory rang, Ken feeling more than a little magnanimous in the glorious aftermath of having just blown, for pure, unadulterated personal pleasure, several thousand pounds of his payment from the Lisbon contract.

Their meeting was memorable for two reasons. One, Ken faced a young man decidedly less confident than when Gregory had quite literally pulled Ken out of the line of fire on their one

and only assignment together. Two, Ken found it hard to believe Gregory's insinuation that Troy Candle had been deep-sixed.

At 11:45 P.M., the moment Gregory became a bloody smear on the tracks of the Hyde Park Underground, Ken Mal dozed in the taxi taking him back to his Radcliffe Garden flat from their meeting.

It was highly unlikely Ken would have learned of Gregory's death if not for a passing remark from Clive Horlson. Gregory's body was well-mangled, and the incident occurred too late to rate more than minimum column-space in the morning newspaper edition that could only reference "an unidentified man." When identification was made, via dental records, Gregory's past connection with several clandestine British-originating intelligence-agency projects, made it convenient that he publically remain permanently anonymous.

Clive, however, wasn't fond of those branches of British Intelligence (or, any other country's intelligence organizations, for that matter) whenever he caught them slamming doors and hiding information.

Certainly, he was no longer as much the pain in the ass for them as he'd once been. In his younger days, he'd gotten hold of a list of British agents in Red China and had begun leaking their names, one by one, to the world press, furious when the sudden disappearances of three of those agents (two more barely having made it out of China alive), saw the British governmental lid come slamming down, by way of complete censorship on that particular Clive-opened Pandora's box. There had been a late-night visit from someone extremely high in the British government who very diplomatically suggested that Clive "mend his ways," offering up a peerage by way of a bribe to make it happen. The result was that all the remaining agent names were kept confidential—much to the relief of the British Foreign Office and to the British moles planted in China.

Of course, Clive refused the peerage, just so he could say one *had* been offered, and he *had* turned it down. When, in fact, he would have probably been far more suited to some baronial

mansion, where he might have wiled away his old age, through association with old horses and old dogs, rather than grow old, as he was, in the flat two floors up from the one Ken was assigned whenever in London.

It was ironic that Clive, a man so caught up in his abhorrence of the spies of his and other countries, couldn't recognize the presence of a safe "house" in his own building, especially since he always passed it whenever headed up the stairs to his own flat. It was merely a case of his being unable to see the forest for the trees. It never crossed his mind that there might be something strange about the different faces he so often glimpsed entering and exiting the place below his at all hours of the day and night. That was because he'd met Ken, during Ken's first stay, had genuinely liked him, and still accepted, at face value, Ken's explanation that he traveled a good deal on business (sales of large farm machinery), and put his flat at the disposal of his company to "put up" visiting dignitaries and representatives from abroad.

Ken was headed out of his door, en route to the corner pharmacy for an aspirin to help soothe his hangover that had resulted from his drinking bout with Gregory the night before, when he ran into Clive coming up the stairs.

"My God, you had best give up that tractor job of yours, my boy, if it makes you look so bloody haggard!" Clive diagnosed, seeing his long-vacant neighbor. "Do come on up for a cuppa tea."

Ken smiled. He had a very pleasant smile, one that dimpled both of his cheeks and immediately belied his thirty-six years to make him look at least ten years younger. He had decidedly boyish good looks, complete with conservatively cut blond hair that banged in a leftward sweep just above his startlingly blue eyes. However, none of that was any more who he really was than was any façade of a motion-picture set that hid all the vacant space behind it. In fact, Ken had never been anyone's typical boy-next-door, even if he had early-on realized the advantages of looking the way he did and in milking them for

everything they were worth.

"In truth, I'm headed on out for an aspirin," Ken said. The way he felt, and Clive's confirmation, were acute overstatements as far as how he actually did look. A more apropos description would have been simply "rumpled and windblown." His blond hair was decidedly tousled. His clothes (not the suit he'd wore the previous evening, but one of the more comfortable throwaways found stuffed in the corner of one dresser) looked as if he might have spent the night sleeping in them. But his tan, gotten in Lisbon, gave him a decidedly healthy glow, as did most tans to light-complexioned people who took to the sun without looking like overly broiled lobsters in result.

"What you really need, then, isn't tea, or an aspirin, but a bit of the hair of the dog!" Clive decided. "If you've drunk yourself out of house and home, you can find all you need, right on up these few stairs. Come on."

Ken really wasn't at all sure that Clive was really right about any alcohol being needed. Ken wasn't a heavy drinker. He'd had way too much with Gregory Ohm, and he knew it. For some reason, being with Gregory had really turned out to be a downer.

Clive recognized a reluctant patient when he saw one, and he proceeded accordingly. He'd spent his morning with an old friend in the medical hierarchy of the New Scotland Yard, and Clive was dying to tell someone about how the government was, once again, trying to hush something up, God only knew why, this time, in that it was that poor sucker who'd "bought it" beneath the subway and had been splattered all over the goddamned tracks the night before. There were people, though, more than prepared to put the bastard in an unmarked grave, even though he was now positively identified. Clive would certainly have made something of it in his younger days. At the present, however, it would suffice for him to bitch about it over a cup of hot Scotch-fortified tea.

"I've, also, aspirin," he enticed, suspecting Ken might be inclined to be saved a trip to the pharmacy. "I've even a few extra I can let you carry away as booty for later."

It was, therefore, over aspirins and drinks, at the little dinette table that Clive had in one corner of his very small kitchen, that Ken learned what had happened to Gregory Ohm shortly after the two had parted company the night before.

CHAPTER FIVE

CAREFULLY, KEN LIFTED the ringing phone and put it to his ear, making doubly sure that he wasn't making himself visible through the window to anyone on the outside.

"Ken, my apologies for the mess," the voice said from the other end of the line. The voice was definitely male, possibly even familiar.

"Who in the hell is this?" Ken hissed. His right hand was sweaty where it gripped his revolver. Whoever the hell it was obviously knew what had been awaiting Ken's arrival at his flat that evening.

"I've made arrangements to send in a cleaning crew," the voice said. "It was thought, however, that it might be better if I called ahead to clear its way."

"I repeat? What in the hell came off here?" Ken asked. He wasn't accustomed to entering his flat and finding a blood-splattered corpse laid out on its living-room rug.

"I'm not quite sure I really know all the details, myself, just yet," the voice replied. Might I suggest that you take a very good look to determine whether or not you can identify."

"I already *have* taken a good look," Ken said. "I *can't* identify."

"Check again on your way out, if you would, please," the voice said. Then, meet me in the bar at Trader Vic's."

"Recognizing you how?"

"I'll find you, Ken, don't worry," the voice said, punctuated with the click as the phone went dead from the other end.

The line, though, wasn't the only thing dead. Once again, Ken checked out the corpse on his floor; definitely, it was beyond revival. He'd already searched its pockets, not having expected to find anything and not having been surprised when he hadn't. If the pockets hadn't arrived empty, they'd likely been emptied by the killer.

Ken would have appreciated some clue—even a little one— to let him know what was happening. He didn't like any of it, coming as it did on the heels of Gregory Ohm's death-by-subway. That Gregory was dead was no longer pure conjecture, either; Ken had contacts at the New Scotland Yard. He'd, also, sent out unsuccessful-so-far feelers to see if anyone knew the present whereabouts of Troy Candle.

He went to the bathroom and washed up, wondering if he should risk walking out and leaving the body on his blood-splattered carpet. He would have all hell to pay if the police got wind of this and came by to do some checking. Of course, he could come up with an alibi to cover his time when the murder had been committed, but walking out without even calling the authorities was liable to go over like a lead balloon if discovered. Still, the voice on the phone sounded competent and in control. Anyway, Ken could hope that was the case. Certainly, he was familiar with traditional clean-up committees—highly specialized teams whose main purpose in life seemed to be death—that had a tendency to show up expected or unexpectedly. There was just the possibility that someone, as insinuated by his caller, would be around to clean up the mess. If that were the case, the quicker the job was done the better off Ken figured he'd be.

He checked the mirror, looking for some visible evidence of the shock he experienced upon entering the flat and finding the body. Aside, though, from his face rather attractively flushed, and his eyes dilated, all likely directly attributable to the flood of adrenaline pumped through his system, he didn't look any the worst for wear. Also, he had somehow miraculously managed to keep any blood off his person. What had been on his hands, he'd

washed off. What had soaked the rug still soaked the rug and was better taken care of by someone expert in removing such stains, or in removing the rug.

He decided to take the chance of getting on the bad side of the police by leaving the scene of the crime. He locked the door behind, having correctly assumed that whoever was sent—if anybody—would hardly be put off by a locked door. Certainly, there as no way that Ken risked any innocent bystander (i.e. Clive Horlson), stumbling in on the mess presently in Ken's living room.

Trader Vic's was in the basement of the Park Lane Hilton. The Hilton wasn't all that far from the Britannia where he'd met up with Gregory for drinks and talked about (the late?) Troy Candle.

He ordered a Scorpion without the gladiola which the London restaurant floated instead of the traditional gardenia that was the garnish of choice everywhere in the States. When his drink arrived, he sipped it; his hangover of a couple nights before was still too vivid a memory for him willingly, quite yet, to welcome any repeat.

He connected the face with the voice on the phone the moment Jerry Crowlson entered the room. Jerry was American. He looked American, too, in the way a well-dressed businessman from somewhere in the Middle West looked stereotypically American. There was simply no way anyone would have mistaken his balding pate, middle-age spread, and capped teeth, for anything but the image Jerry tried so hard, and so successfully, to portray. Few people would have suspected, just by looking, that Jerry, on the payroll of the American Embassy, as a foreign-affairs consultant, was one of the best CIA operatives the U.S. had in Europe. Ken had had brief dealing with him three years previously when the U.S. was anxious to obtain coordinates to a North Korean submarine gone down in international waters, code books aboard.

"Glad you could make it," Jerry said, sitting down. One of the waiters followed him to the table, and Jerry ordered a double

Scotch, turning back to Ken as soon as the waiter faded back into the woodwork. "I hope you like brown rugs."

Ken couldn't immediately figure out the reference and showed as much by his expression. Jerry laughed.

"We're providing you with a new carpet for your flat," Jerry qualified. "Our friend was quite the bleeder. Were you able, by the way, to make a belated ID?"

Ken shook his head.

"Oh, well, we'll run what we have through our computers and hope something turns up." Jerry said. "We might get lucky."

"Right now, I'd settle for just hearing what that dead man is doing in my flat," Ken said, taking another sip of his pleasantly tart drink.

"Actually, I had come by for a little chat with you, and, suddenly, there he was, gun in hand" Jerry surprised. "Had I been any less coordinated, it would have been my body awaiting your arrival. I rather doubt your other guest would have been nearly as obliging about cleaning up his mess. If I were you, by the way, I would be most careful, just in case there is one or more of the same ilk lurking thereabouts."

"A person makes enemies in our business," Ken reminded. His hackneyed statement didn't explain anything, and both men knew it. Jerry, though, let it pass without comment. For the life of him, Ken couldn't imagine why he was suddenly on anyone's hit list. The most suspect, at the moment, would be his most recent employers on the Lisbon job, but he'd left them, by their own admissions, exceptionally well satisfied. That particular project, in fact, had gone with surprisingly few hitches; certainly none which warranted orders to see Ken permanently out of the way.

Jerry took another swallow of his Scotch.

"My sources tell me you're presently available for employment," he said, eyeing Ken over the edge of his glass.

"I just finished an assignment," Ken said, "which leaves me rather desirous of taking a few weeks off."

"From what I hear, the Lisbon deal wasn't all that taxing."

"Lisbon?" Ken asked, trying to sound all innocence. He had no doubt, however, that Jerry was well-informed.

"We're having a few problems," Jerry said, getting to the point. He knew all he wanted to know about the Lisbon deal; if he didn't already have the information, he rightly figured Ken wouldn't likely volunteer it. It wasn't what happened in Lisbon which interested Jerry, anyway. What *did* interest him was the fate of several missing independent Grey Zone agents. If Jerry hadn't known better, he would have suspected Ken was one of those independents suddenly marked "to become missing", too. So far, though, Ken's death wouldn't fit the existent *modus operandi*. Most of those missing had worked far more closely with America than Ken ever had.

"What problems?" Ken asked, well aware there was a regular contingent of independent Grey Zone agents, other than him, to whom American intelligence usually turned when commissioning anything out-of-house.

"Several often-used-by-us Grey Zone assets have recently come up missing," Jerry said. "We're looking for someone, positioned as you are, and not regularly called upon by us, to check around and see if you can find out why."

Ken had never been fond of dealing with the Americans, which is why he so seldom had. He'd found their operations, for the most part, way often too sloppy to suit his sensibilities.

Jerry's thoughts turned, and not for the first time, to the dead man he'd left in Ken's flat. If Jerry had that scenario right—and he thought that he did—Ken's life expectancy might not be any longer than any of those men within the usual pool of independent Grey Zone agents from which the U.S. drew; Jerry had expressed just that opinion to his superiors who had discarded it. There was, they pointed out, always the possibility the now-dead assassin in Ken's apartment hadn't been out to get Ken, at all, but to get Jerry who might have been followed there. As Ken had so succinctly noted: Enemies were easily made in their business, no matter which side, even in-between.

Ken and Jerry discussed finances; Ken, in the end, was

more persuaded by the money offered than by any real desire to help. Jerry would have liked Ken more enthusiastic but had to be content with what he got. After all, he was pretty sure Ken wasn't the only Grey Zone base being touched in an effort to determine the reason or reasons behind the sudden rash of missing American-affiliated Grey Zone freelance agents. If Ken was the only contact being brought in, Jerry suspected there would have been a bit more reaction from Jerry's superiors to the dead man Jerry had left in Ken's living room.

"So, how about specifics?" Ken asked. He'd ordered another drink, this time a Perrier.

"Three Grey Zone freelance agents who have frequently worked closely with us are suddenly disappeared without a trace."

"Names?" Ken wasn't taking notes on paper, but he was committing everything to memory. He'd learned a long time ago that things written on paper were too easily misplaced, and, then, way too easily found by the competition or by the enemy.

"Denver Rheingold," Jerry said, "last seen in Rome. Johan Darnel, last seen in Paris, with a possible sighting on a Paris-Amsterdam train. Troy Candle, last involved in something 'Libyan', since reported as missing-in-action."

"Troy Candle?" Ken asked.

"That rings bells, does it?" Jerry asked. He'd dealt with enough people to read inflection in the voice of someone who knew something. Of course, Candle had been a very well-known active within the Grey Zone intelligence-gathering arena.

"You might want to check Egypt to see if Candle is there," Ken answered.

"You have reason to believe he is?" It seemed logical that an agent involved in Libya might possibly have been sent for espionage purposes into Egypt. If that were the case, it would have certainly behooved the Libyans to let leak Candle had disappeared, especially if his presence ever turned up across the border.

"I have reason to believe that he might well have been

murdered there," Ken said, sipping more of his Perrier and carefully noting Jerry's reaction.

CHAPER SIX

THERE ARE EASY ways to pass through airport customs, even in cities like Cairo, where miles of red tape and rows of bureaucrats seem determined to make absolutely nothing easy. Two methods are readily available to the average tourist. For liberal out-of-pocket monetary hand-outs, *bakkish,* seemingly helplessly rusty gears can be made to turn more smoothly. And/ or, if you're prepared to travel with the bare minimum of carry-on, you won't have to wait for baggage to be time-consumingly hauled out of the plane and be gone over by customs and airport security. Of course, the latter might well act to your detriment, rather than to your benefit, especially if you're looking a bit seedy, as do the majority of travelers, usually young, out for maximum itinerary flexibility. Youth provides the stamina to survive alien and exotic climes and cultures, but, when combined with relaxed dress standards, and few bags, often ties someone up (literally) for long-long periods in any airport as security-conscious as the one servicing Cairo.

Best for entering a country hassle-free is with a diplomatic passport. While more secrets to the detriment of a host country are passed in and out of areas via the sacrosanct confines of a diplomatic pouch, than ever went out taped to the ribs of some vagabond traveler, all forms of bullshit are done away with if you arrive pre-armed with the right paperwork.

Ken arrived with all three easements in his favor. If he wasn't personally crossing palms with silver (in this case with Egyptian pound notes), there had been people there, well before him,

liberally slathering on monetary lubricant. He arrived with only one bag, his carry-on attaché case, which, among other things, contained a change of shirt, socks, and underwear. He entered under the protective umbrella of diplomatic immunity. His passport was American, with attending paperwork that confirmed his temporary "attachment" to the American Embassy, Cairo.

Checked in at the Hilton, he scoped his room for exits, in case a speedy one was ever necessary. He checked for electronic bugs; if he couldn't be completely trusted by his American employers, he wasn't prepared to trust them completely, either.

He didn't bother stepping out on the balcony to admire the view. He'd seen it all before and was jaded to most exotic sights and sounds that would trigger any average tourist to spout enough adjectives to fill a thesaurus.

He slept, no counting of sheep necessary, no intermittent periods of insomnia, no need for a sleeping pill. He was simply asleep the minute his head hit the pillow. It had nothing to do with his plush accommodations. He would have fallen asleep just as easily if holed up for the night on some rocky mountainside. It all had to do with his training and the nature of his job. If he didn't catch what sleep he could, when he could, even in the oddest of moments, he would soon have succumbed to exhaustion—in more ways than one. An exhausted man was a careless man. And, in Ken's business, more often than not, a careless man was a dead one.

If his sleep wasn't sound (more that of a cat than of a hibernating bear), that didn't mean it wasn't sufficient. He had been without "normal" sleep for so long that he'd forgotten what it was. Thus, he hardly missed something unremembered.

The next morning, his night having been uninterrupted by anything that had automatically keyed him into immediate wakefulness and counteractive measures, he felt refreshed, made more so by taking a shower that at no time put his weapon out of reach.

He paid little narcissistic attention to his naked body reflected by the bathroom mirrors. If he was in exceptionally good phys-

ical condition, it was because he treated his body no more nor less than it deserved as a finely tuned implement obviously best prepared to serve him if in its prime. It was a vital piece of his arsenal; he would no more have been neglectful of its upkeep than he would have shirked on the maintenance of any weapon needed for an assignment.

Of course, he could have been full of self-loving if he ever had a mind to. His body was the kind most men dreamed of having, but few men had. It wasn't bulky, like a body builder's, but its muscle definition was nonetheless there, chiseled to perfection on a physique that seemed entirely cast in bronze except for the white swimming-trunk line around his hips, at the vee of his crotch, and down the crack of his ass.

At six-feet-one, he had square pectorals covered with fine blond hair which appeared even blonder against the darkness of his tan. His stomach was wash-boarded horizontal ripples punctuated, here and there, by vertical ridges. His arms and legs were well-muscled and relayed animal grace whenever he was in movement.

He dressed, then left the hotel for breakfast, all of the while trying to pinpoint any tails. He knew they'd be there, and he soon had four spotted. Not that they went to any great lengths to keep their presence a secret, which indicated their momentary friendliness. They knew that he knew that they were part of the game. They were there as much for his protection as to keep him from getting up to no good.

He spent most of the rest of his day wandering busy and crowded Cairo streets, making neither rhyme nor reason of his meandering so no one could detect a pattern and take advantage. He was prepared to take all possible precautions to cover his ass. If Gregory Ohm's death had something to do with Ohm's assassination of Troy Candle, it was logical that the closer Ken got to the "why" of Candle's assassination, the closer he came to being offed himself. If—as evidenced by his own lucky escape from the mysterious killer who Jerry Crowlson had obligingly dispatched—he wasn't already contracted for termination

At six o'clock, he was back at the Nile Hilton, and gave a bellboy his key with instructions to bring his attaché case down to the lobby. Once he had the case in his hand, he took a cab to the Cairo Railway Station at Midan Ramses. He already had his train ticket for the MBB sleeper to Aswan, given him by the driver of the Mercedes who had initially driven him into town from the airport. All of which, once again, proved there were benefits to being a visiting VIP. Usually, purchases of train tickets required a face-to-face with officials at stations, accompanied by the presentation of a passport and much resulting paperwork. For night trains, reservations were often needed as much as a week in advance.

He was allowed entrance to railroad car 1, cabins 1 and 2, immediately upon arrival. He requested and got an immediate turning down of his bed, declining the offer for the dinner to be served at eight-thirty.

By the time the train left the station, beginning its fifteen-hour race, south, to Aswan, Ken was asleep, his automatic firearm clutched in his hand beneath his pillow.

CHAPTER SEVEN

"I CAN'T BELIEVE THIS!" Jerry Crowlson said. That really wasn't true, but it certainly didn't make him any less indignant; he'd witnessed enough screw-ups in his lifetime to know there was nothing all that exceptional about this one.

"What's not to be believed?" Eldridge Filholden asked from the opposite end of the conference table. Actually, he could very well see why Jerry might be disturbed. Eldridge knew that, had he been in Jerry's shoes, he would have probably been just as indignant. "I thought I made everything perfectly clear."

"What you did was leave out a good many goddamned details!" Jerry accused. If this smug bastard thought he was getting away with this bullshit without Jerry persuading him to shed a bit more light on the subject, he was sadly mistaken

"National security, and all of that," Eldridge said with an expression that indicated he would be more than happy to spill his guts if —IF—it wasn't simply impossible for him to do so.

Jerry, though, wasn't buying it.

"You expect us simply to abort, because *you* say so?

"Not because *I* say so," Eldridge reminded. "Jesus, who am I? Who are any of us, for that matter?"

"Come off the bullshit rhetoric!" Jerry demanded.

Eldridge, though, had to fall back on something. It wasn't as if he had a choice. Hell, if he'd had his way, he might very well tell Jerry everything. Or, if not everything—not even Eldridge knew *everything*—he, at the very least, would have told Jerry all Eldridge knew. Eldridge, though, had his instructions rooted

firmly within the age-old push-and-pull groundwork that was forever ongoing on between U.S. sister intelligence agencies (hell, the agencies really didn't even have to be *intelligence*). Every one of which had its own little realm of influence and didn't want any one stumbling on over into it. The problem, of course, was how just such lack of communication often allowed such interference to occur when it probably wouldn't have if lines of communication had merely been a little less clogged by friction and petty jealousies in the first place.

"I do understand your chagrin," Eldridge said, prepared to be magnanimous. "However, I'm afraid that, the way things stand, you simply don't have a need to know."

Need to know was another of those catch-all phrases, like *national security*, given as a reason for some course of action; really no goddamned answer at all.

"I want to know what in the hell is coming off here!" Jerry insisted, simultaneously knowing that he was probably beating a dead horse. He would probably save himself one helluva lot of bother by sitting back and accepting that somewhere, somehow, his intelligence agency had moved into an area of conflicting interest with another on-the-same-side intelligence agency.

"It's not, after all, as if we're on opposite teams, is it?" Eldridge reminded.

Jerry had a sarcastic comment ready for that one—something to the effect that he wasn't at all sure they *were* on the same side—but he bit his tongue. Inter- and intra-agency squabbles did far more harm than they ever did good.

"Now, *is it?*" Eldridge insisted, knowing full well what Jerry was thinking. Eldridge thought the very same on more than one occasion in the past. However, he wasn't about to admit to that. Despite what he thought, he had to maintain at least the illusion of cooperation. This was simply the way the game was played. If Jerry's tail was in a kink, now, because he was instructed, without adequate explanation, to pull away from some area, then, he would undoubtedly have the satisfaction, before too many moons passed, of telling Eldridge, or Eldridge's parent

company, to pull away from somewhere else. Turnabout was fair play. The same thing that happened in this American Embassy room, today, happened all of the time, in all of the rooms up and down this corridor. Eldridge knew that, and Jerry knew that. In the end, all of this in-between stuff was merely superfluous horseshit.

"I just wish it could be made clearer to me why," Jerry said. "Those missing independent Grey Zone agents were important to my organization. It's important that we find out who took them out of operation. We have spent a good deal of time, effort, and money trying to do just that. To simply call us off, now, because of your say-so...."

"Not *my* say-so, *do, please*, remember," Eldridge interrupted. "Never *my* say so. You have noted the signature at the bottom of the directive, have you not?"

Yes, Jerry had read the signature on the directive. Eldridge *knew* he had read the signature on the directive.

"It's all been decided at higher echelons," Eldridge said soothingly. "I'm merely the messenger. All of the why and the why-not have been laid out on some tabletop and analyzed by others with higher pay-grades. I can only assure you that the final decision wasn't made without a good deal of thought. In time, the reasoning, I'm sure, will filter down to both of us, making everything crystal clear."

"Bullshit!" Jerry said.

Eldridge thought Jerry's response certainly apropos for the statements Eldridge had just delivered with such a straight face. However, bullshit or not, didn't change anything. Anyway, knowing answers didn't always make things any better; it often made things worse. Better to be kept in the dark than be made privy to every detail behind every major or minor fuck-up. Details could unnerve a person and make him or her begin to doubt the capacity of superiors to handle the mechanisms that made the world go round.

"Bullshit or not, you will comply, yes?" Eldridge said, gathering his papers into a pile and tapping their lower edges against

the tabletop to align them neatly.

Jerry frowned, crossed his arms over his chest, and gave all appearance that he wasn't about to be bullied into anything. On the other hand, he knew he had lost. Eldridge knew Jerry had lost. Why in the hell were they wasting valuable time and valuable energy?

"I don't like it," Jerry said and, then, repeated the very same statement.

"You have our assurance that successful access will soon be opened to you, once again, into the existing pool of independent freelance agents within the Grey Zone," Eldridge said.

"Yes, I know that's what the paper insinuates," Jerry said. "What I'm wondering, though, is how your people can make any such promise? Or, are you the ones who fucked us to begin with?"

"It's all available on a need-to-know basis," Eldridge said, sticking his papers in their file folder.

The session was over. Decisions had been made. There was nothing Jerry Crowlson could do but comply, even if he did find it all pretty goddamned fishy.

CHAPTER EIGHT

KEN'S REFLEXES WERE HONED to perfection, or he would have probably come out the worse, even with the warning "Watch out!" which put him on guard. As it was, he turned just in time to counter the knife thrust coming at him from behind at just the right angle that, had he not successfully countered, would likely have seen him just as dead as the man he'd come to Tomb 42 in Aswan to investigate.

The knife point hooked his shirt, where material bloused slightly at the waistband of his trousers, no immediate evidence of even a flesh wound resulting. Ken would swear, though, to having actually felt the coolness of well-tempered steel in its glide across his taut belly.

What happened next was unclear, reflexively programmed as it was by pure animal instinct, rather than by any conscious preconceived play-by-play of anticipated moves and counter-moves. It merely registered in Ken's mind, for dead certain, that his life was in danger, and his body, from then on out, moved on automatic.

Not that he would have survived the attack, even then, if it wasn't for additional assistance from the merciful angel who put him aware of the assassination attempt in the first place. It was quickly evident that the knife-wielding Arab was an expert, even if momentarily frustrated by Ken's turn and defensive parry. The attacker quickly recovered, more than ready to initiate whatever additional moves needed to rectify an objective temporarily thwarted.

The Arab, having lost his advantage of surprise, still had the obvious advantage of familiar surroundings. The light from Ken's flashlight, which was extinguished at the same time Ken dropped it and turned to face his opponent, didn't reappear during the course of the scuffle. Ken had visions of his attacker toppling him into one of the deep pits that pockmarked the tomb's interior.

If, somewhere, in the back of his mind, Ken heard and recognized the popping retort of a weapon fired through a muffling silencer, he couldn't possibly be sure the resulting bullets weren't aimed at him. Even the dead-weight suddenly atop him, the body of the Arab who had accepted the slugs like a sponge taking on water, didn't offer any immediately conclusive assurances. The Arab might be dead merely because, in the darkness of the tomb, someone had misaimed and dispatched the wrong target.

"Ken, are you okay?" a voice asked. A flashlight was clicked on and swung so its beam isolated the body of the Arab sprawled on Ken in the dust.

Ken quickly scooted from beneath the man and ensconced himself behind one of the pillars that gave the illusion of supporting what was actually a free-standing ceiling. He could have easily taken a bead on the light, and quickly dispatched the person at the other end. He was stopped by his continuing awareness that someone *had* warned him about, and, then, *had* killed the Arab.

"I've my gun drawn," Ken warned. "So, why don't you slowly aim that light to show me your face? No funny moves unless you'd like to join our friend, there, in Kingdom-come."

The beam of the flashlight slowly trailed off the body on the tomb floor and angled upward to form a column of white that dead-ended on the rock to form a full moon on the ceiling. As Ken instructed, a face was soon thrust into the illuminating pillar.

"Dilah Sleene?" he asked, immediately recognizing the face but hardly believing. The last time he'd seen her was in

Istanbul, five years before. He'd since heard rumors (one was always hearing rumors in the trade), that she'd been killed in El Salvador during an attempted communist coup.

"You really don't think I would have gone to the bother of, one, warning you, and, two, killing your proposed killer for you, do you, if I were planning to make some kind of an attempt on your life?" the attractive woman asked the obvious.

And, it *was* Dilah, all right. There was no mistaking her sultry voice, coming as it did from her face made exotically attractive by high cheekbones, slightly slanted eyes, and sensuously full lips. The body that went with that face and voice, although presently shrouded in darkness, was, unless it had changed since Ken had last seen it, just as exquisite.

"Right now, I'm a little unsure what to believe," Ken said. "Understandable, yes?"

"Understandable, by all means," Dilah agreed." So, why don't we move a little closer to the door and take advantage of the light, there, that will assure you that I have no intentions of trying anything funny?"

"Very well," Ken said. "Since you have the flashlight, what say you lead the way?"

"My pleasure," Dilah agreed. If she was well aware that she had just been responsible for leaving one very dead attempted-assassin sprawled in the sand, that awareness wasn't reflected by any trace of hysteria in her voice. But, then, as Ken well remembered, Dilah was never one to let a simple termination rile her.

He watched her trail of light slowly recede from him, and he memorized its pathway to the door. He didn't immediately follow, however, taking his time, instead, to visually survey his surroundings for any indications that there might be more than just the two of them left alive within the tomb complex.

"There is no one else in here," Dilah called back, moving in to the daylight that was spilling through the doorway. Obviously she'd identified the reasons that had delayed him in immediately following her.

By then, pretty much convinced that her statement was true, Ken followed more quickly, especially careful not to step into any holes; he felt pretty sure he knew how to run the gauntlet of pitfalls between himself and Dilah at the doorway.

He didn't holster his gun even after he reached her and re-verified that she was who she said she was.

"Come on, now, Ken," Dilah cajoled. "You must know how nervous it makes me to stare down the barrel of any loaded gun."

Her own gun, its silencer unscrewed and stored in the pocket of her bush jacket, was deposited within its holster that rode her right hip.

"I thought you were dead in El Salvador," he said, remembering the tinge of actual emotion he'd allowed himself upon getting word of her possible death during that bloody revolution.

"Someone obviously inflated his or her death count," she said, a smile playing on her full lips. "Are you happy I survived?"

"You saved my life just now, did you not?" Ken said. "You would have been hard-pressed to perform such a service had you been a corpse."

Dilah laughed. She had a way of making herself sound as if she was genuinely amused by what he said. Ken knew, though, that she was a consummate actress.

"Shall we talk, then?" she asked, leaning against one cut-rock doorjamb. "Or, would you rather we just admired the view that includes each other and the dead man just inside?"

The vista from the opening was, indeed, spectacular. The escarpment, into which all of the tombs of the nobles were carved, overlooked a stretch of the Nile; the Hotel Oberoi on Elephantine Island was mid-river; the modern city of Aswan, readily identified by the minarets of its mosque, climbed the oppose embankment and hillside.

"I hope this doesn't sound as if I'm unappreciative," Ken said, deciding that had Dilah wanted him dead, she could have let the Arab take care of him, or she could have killed Ken, not the Arab, while the two men scuffled, "but wouldn't it have

been easier for you immediately to have dispatched our friend, in there, rather than waste time screaming me a warning? If I remember correctly, you've always been a crack shot, and if there was enough light available for you to see what was being attempted, there should have been enough to get an aim on that bastard to kill him, all without waiting for my macho display of wrestling skills to manhandle him to the ground."

"Don't you think you're rather looking this gift horse in the mouth?" Dilah asked. Her smile was wide, revealing her exceptionally white teeth.

"It's not that I don't thank you for what you did, but…."

Perhaps I don't have the reflexes I did when I was younger?" Dilah suggested. "Perhaps I couldn't trust myself to put the bullet in a place that would stop his momentum. I've known wounded men, after all, who could still function as deadly weapons after being the victims of even eventually fatal wounds."

"Perhaps," Ken said, although he doubted the validity of either alternative she'd provided.

"Or, maybe my hesitation was born from a need to let you come to a quick realization as to just what kind of a dangerous situation you were in, and still are in?" she suggested. The tomb, on the West bank of the Nile, faced East into the sun. Although it was still early morning, it was warm. "Had I shot the Arab right off, how would you really have known he was about to make an attempt on your life?"

"How do I know you didn't put him up to it in the first place?" Ken asked. "Maybe, you staged this little rescue charade to impress me?"

"And you're impressed, are you?" Dilah asked.

"I'd be even more impressed if I knew for sure it hadn't been planned totally for my benefit," Ken said.

"Who was it who introduced you to the Arab in question?" Dilah asked; this time, it was a wry smile that played across her sensuous lips. "I?"

"Hardly," Ken admitted. "I thought you were dead in El Salvador."

"Who, then?" she persisted. "Some official attached to some foreign government? Mine?"

Glenn Jargreave, Ken's American contact in Aswan, had made the introduction that had assigned Ken to the Arab's safe-keeping for the morning trip to the site of the Troy Candle's murder. Glenn was Jerry Crowlson' man in Egypt.

"You see, then, what I'm getting at?" Dilah asked, sensing Ken was smart enough to reason it out.

Why would the Americans want me dead?" Ken asked. "They just hired me."

"There was merely a lack of U.S. inter-agency communication as regarded your hiring," Dilah said. "We both know what an octopus the American intelligence service is, don't we? "Denver Rheingold, Johan Darnel, and Troy Candle. Remember them?"

"Get to the point, will you?"

"How about Gregory Ohm?"

"Come on, Dilah," Ken insisted. "Why don't you just spit out whatever it is you have to say to me?"

"They were all ordered killed by a branch of U.S. intelligence."

"Go on."

"The branch in question is concerned with special projects, one of which required the services of agents who, if caught, in the act, couldn't automatically be identified as 'belonging to' the U.S. side. Thus, some fishing was done in the Grey Zone for three independent agents who had been 'used' surreptitiously by Americans before, but who, also, had been used by so many others, too, that there seemed little danger of any immediate U.S.-connect. Namely, Rheingold, Darnel, and Candle, used, and, then, eliminated to assure no leads-back to the U.S. who hired them. After all, that's not something we haven't heard of happening before, is it, under one guise or another; those of you within the Grey Zone, with no particular life-time allegiances, are often considered acceptable collateral damage, yes?"

"What kind of U.S. project are you talking?" Ken asked. He

followed where she was taking him, all right, but there were still a helluva lot of pitfalls in the walkway.

"Meanwhile," Dilah said, having decided to ignore Ken's question for the moment and get on with the direction she preferred," there was the CIA, that most well-known branch of U.S. Intelligence, whose previous use of Candle, Rheingold, and Darnel, was what caused that trio to be on the government computer reads-out for the Grey Zone to begin with. Suddenly, the CIA realized three of its key links to the freelance community were missing. The special projects operation of its sister group was so secret that not even the CIA had a clue; so CIA people became damned paranoid and damned curious as to what was happening. At which point, you were called in by them, because you have good contacts, among your fellow freelancers in the Grey Zone, and it was thought you might possibly shed some light on the seeming mystery."

Whether any, or all, of that was bullshit, it seemed within the realm of possibility—at least so far. The best lies, though, were always the ones that didn't sound like lies, because they were so close to the truth.

"What about Gregory Ohm?" Ken asked.

"When the U.S. special-projects group decided Candle, Rheingold, and Darnel, had to be killed, Ohm was contracted to kill Candle. After which, he, of course, was murdered when it was figured he may have passed on information in an untimely meeting he had with you. That's why you, in turn, ended up a target."

That, Ken thought, could explain Jerry Crowlson having inadvertently blown away a fellow U.S. intelligence agent, in Ken's apartment, before having been made privy to Ken having been targeted by a sister intelligence agency on Crowlson's own side.

"And, how, may I ask, did you become the recipient of all this insider information?" Ken asked. However she had managed it, if it was true, Ken was suddenly more than a little appreciative. If Dilah hadn't been there, waiting for him in Tomb 42, there

was a good chance he, and not the Arab, would now be dead and lying face down in the dust formed by generations of wind-blown sand.

"I didn't become privy to it overnight, and not without a good deal of difficulty, you can bet you handsome muscled ass on that," Dilah said. "In fact, some of it was damned hard to come by, paid for with cash, services, and at least one of my fellow Russian agent's life."

"This does, I hope, bring us to just what it all boils down to by way of end game."

Unlike Ken, Dilah wasn't a Grey Zone free agent who took jobs from whichever side happened to be offering the most money at any one time. She was under Soviet employ, and had been since before the fall of USSR Empire. So, unless that had changed since he'd last seen her...

"Undoubtedly, you've heard of the incident at Brimzinsky?" Dilah asked. She crossed her arms across her ample breasts and took a quick look over the sun-shimmering Nile valley toward the dusty city on the other side. It was doubtful, though, she was aware of the beauty of the scene. She turned her attention back to Ken.

"This has something to do with Brimzinsky?" he asked. Sure, he'd heard of it. Who hadn't?

Brimzinsky was (rather, *had been*) a village in Siberia, set within a stretch of nondescript land of little apparent note, originally assumed near no military bases, or missile silos, or industry, merely ice, snow, and deep-set permafrost. Suddenly, all of its people and livestock turned up dead. Pressured by the Free World, amid accusations of a radioactive or biological accident, the Russians still publically insisted, without allowing any close scrutiny by outsiders, that the incident at Brimzinsky was nothing but freakish (even for Siberia) cold-weather spasms having caused a mass extinction. Recently revised maps had simply eliminated any indication that Brimzinsky ever existed.

"Well?" Ken asked finally. For a moment, he wondered whether or not Dilah was going to continue.

"It wasn't bad weather that killed the residents of Brimzinsky."

"No shit, Sherlock!" Ken said in mock surprise. "Who would have ever guessed?" His voice dripped sarcasm.

"The incident was the result of a U.S. biological agent released on the site."

"What?" There was no way Ken swallowed that major assertion merely on Dilah's say-so. More likely, Brimzinsky, people and livestock, were knocked out, if not by the up-until-now-Russian-accused storm, then, by some horrendous Russian-brewed concoction conjured by Russian scientists in some Russian laboratory hidden in that frozen Russian landscape. Not that the U.S. didn't likely have its own incubators filled to the brim with all kinds of new and deadly germ varieties, but....

Dilah having sensed his doubt might well have caused the obvious darkening of her expression, as well as the anger in her voice as she continued.

"Yes, you heard me correctly!" she insisted. "A fatal *U.S.-grown* bacteria, Zilinium-40, clandestinely hand-carried into Russia by Candle, Rheingold, and Darnel, under direct instruction from America, in order to damage Russia's world-wide credibility by making it look as if we continue experimental germ warfare, despite all existent treaties signed to specifically prohibit us from doing so."

"Even if I were to make the huge leap of faith that required I assume any of this as true..." Ken left the rest unsaid

"It recently came to our attention, via certain materials attained, clandestinely, from U.S. sources, that all three Grey Area agents involved in the delivery of the U.S.-manufactured toxin to Brimzinsky received pre-delivery inoculations to keep them from dying, along with everyone and everything else at the drop site, if, God-forbid, they were exposed during delivery. If that's the case, traces of that antidote, as well as the poison from which it was derived, are permanently present within each agent's physical make-up. If we can get hold of one or more of those men, connect them to a toxin that remains supposedly indicative solely of Brimzinsky, nowhere else...then, link one

or more of inoculated agents to the U.S. government…we'll pretty much have proof that what happened at Brimzinsky was a set-up that had nothing to do with Russian biological or radioactive experimentation. Unfortunately, recent events indicate the Americans know what we know and are moving fast, after the fact, to keep us from doing what we're so intent upon doing."

"The Americans mean to kill off Candle, Darnel, and Rheingold, before you can access them, you mean?"

"We figure that by our having you along for the ride, what with your contacts within the freelance Grey Zone community, we'll have a better chance of locating Rheingold and Darnel if they, unlike Candle, are still alive."

"And, that's why you saved me?" Ken divined.

"That—among other reasons," Dilah argreed.

CHAPTER NINE

"DON'T WORRY," DILAH SAID. "These people have done this sort of thing for centuries. Even King Tut's tomb showed evidence of grave robbers having been there. And that's the only royal tomb that came through with even part of its valuables intact."

Ken smiled wryly at Dilah's attempted simile. He pulled the collar of his jacket closer around his neck, and not only because it got so damned cold in such a bleak desert landscape incapable of retaining any day's generous heat after sunset.

There was a thin slice of moon rising on the horizon. Aside from that, the only light was supplied by lamps around the supposed designated grave site and by stars twinkling brightly in the inky heavens above.

Something about the whole scene seemed ghoulish. Something about the whole scene *was* ghoulish. Ken couldn't shake childhood chills experienced while watching Dr. Frankenstein (or, was it his assistant, Igor?) rifling graves for pieces of corpses with which to put together a monster. All sorts of other childhood horrors seemed associated with graveyards, too; zombies, and vampires, for instance. Fortunately, Ken was a child no longer!

"Are you worried someone might catch us?" Dilah asked. "Frankly, I would be a bit more encouraged if there *were* a few guards posted in the area."

"How do I even know this is where Troy Candle is buried?" Ken asked.

"If you wish to take the time, I'm sure can verify, to your satisfaction, through contacts of your own, that this is where Egyptian authorities decided to put his remains."

There was the sudden sound of a spade hitting wood that, as far as Ken was concerned, might just as well have been a fingernail across a blackboard.

"Sounds like someone just hit pay dirt," Dilah said, putting her hand on Ken's sleeve. "Shall we move a little closer and see with what rewards, if any, this night is about to grace us?"

Ken moved forward with her, standing on the edge of the grave. Arab workmen, knee deep in loose earth, used cupped hands to scoop the remaining dirt off the wooden coffin lid.

Ken told himself that there was no reason to feel the way he was feeling. After all, it wasn't as if he hadn't seen a dead man before. Hell, he'd seen more people to the grave, in one way or another, than probably filled many a good-size cemetery. He had seen people killed one at a time, two at a time, three at a time, and en masse. Corpses weren't novelties to him any longer. If this one was at all different, it was only because it was the first Ken had actually helped disinter.

Not that there was necessarily anything in the coffin. In fact, Dilah had just about assured him there likely wouldn't be.

"The Americans wouldn't take the chance of leaving it lying around, even below ground, where someone, like me, with a clue, could get my hands on it, would they?" she'd conjectured.

Ken hadn't asked the, then, superfluous question—"So, why even bother disturbing the grave?"—because he knew the answer. Actually, there were at least two reasons. One, there was just the possibility that the Americans had been careless, thinking Candle's secret safe with him, when buried six feet under. If that were the case, it would have been ridiculous for the Russians to overlook that possibility. Two, if the body wasn't there, that would be one more finger pointing toward cover-up shenanigans in progress.

"Open the lid!" Dilah instructed the local helpers.

Ken felt the shudder run through him, hoping against hope

that the body wouldn't be there. Not so much because he wanted more circumstantial evidence of U.S. involvement in the Brimzinsky Incident, but because he didn't relish the idea of a body, throat slit, that wouldn't look any too appetizing under the best of circumstances.

An Arab disengaged the coffin lid with expertise that bespoke, as Dilah had insinuated, a history of prowling graves, past and present, for possible valuables any deceased had foolishly thought to take with him to the afterworld.

The coffin was empty.

"Empty!" Ken verified, as if saying so made it more so.

"Of course," Dilah said and had no further use for the place. She gave Ken's arm a gentle tug that took him off the mound of freshly turned earth and moved him toward the Land Rover in the shadows. They left those who, having manually dug up the grave for money-paid would, now, re-fill it for the same.

Ken was naturally skittish, checking each and every shadow for a figure crouching within it. He wasn't made easier by his Aswan U.S. contact, Glenn Jargreave, likely knowing, by now, that something unscheduled had taken place in Tomb 42. Even if Jargreave wouldn't find the Arab's body, Dilah having assured Ken that such evidence of murder would be removed, there would be no dead Ken there, either. Jargreave would have gotten word of that to his superiors, and shit would undoubtedly have hit the fan.

Jargreave's superiors would have every reason to be upset by this latest turn of events. It was one thing for them to catch Ken unaware and kill him. It was quite another to kill him once he was actually expecting an attempt and watched for it. By failing, the bastards had, also, succeeded in making themselves one hell of an enemy, especially now that Ken was teamed with Dilah, yet another enemy of America on the game board.

Ken did have connections available for helping the Russians locate the other two missing agents. If three freelancers had been utilized in a clandestine operation by some special group of U.S. Intelligence, and spread some kind of U.S.-made bacterial

agent at Brimzinsky, their ordered terminations connected to all of that, Ken, clues now in hand, was better able to check it out than was any agent solely connected to Russia or to America. If countries kept extensive files on their own agents, and files on enemy agents, Grey Area freelance agents often kept files of their own that might later be used as leverage within that murky Grey-Zone world in which they existed. Yes, by God, Ken had sources from which to draw. He had every intention of doing so, too. If, as it looked, the Americans had set him up for murder, as but one more attempt to cover their dirty tracks to, at, and from Brimzinsky, they were going to be very sorry. Ken's need for righteous indignation and vengeance was enhanced by the substantial monetary rewards Dilah's side unashamedly offered him, and he unabashedly accepted.

They reached the car and got in. Dilah put the vehicle into gear and headed off into the desert, leaving the headlights off.

"Where to now?" Ken asked. Certainly, it would behoove them to leave Egypt as quickly as possible.

"Where do you think?" Dilah was positive that Ken saw the writing on the wall as well as she did.

"Out of Egypt, I can only hope," he said, once again marveling at how a desert so hot during the day could be so cold after dark.

"Yes, definitely out of Egypt," Dilah agreed. "I think, possibly, we might best check out the present possible where-abouts of Darnel and Rheingold, dead or alive, utilizing your European Grey Zone contacts, and do so on-site in Europe."

Although she left the car lights off, Dilah continued to give the impression that she knew where she was driving. Ken, though, jokingly made it a point to ask, just to make sure.

"We Russians built the High Dam for these people, remember?" Dilah reminded. "If anyone is familiar with the terrain around here, I assure you it's someone, like me, who has made extensive use of records and maps our advisory teams brought home with them when they were so rudely kicked out of here."

They drove into deeper desert, leaving behind all signs of

modern civilization.

The moon crawled higher up the horizon, its milky silver fading the light of those stars immediately clustered around it; the rest of the night sky continued to sparkle ice-cold brilliance.

The landscape included rose-tinted granite gravel and deep drifts of tan sand. This was the Sahara, with, as far as Ken knew, nothing between them and the Red Sea but a mountain range that ran parallel to the coastline, and, thus, offered barrier after barrier to the nearest-seaport of Berenice. Even if the terrain allowed easier access to the sea, the Rover didn't have nearly enough gas in its tank to make the trip.

Dilah continued to seem confident about the outcome of their escape in progress, seemingly little worried that it was probable as all hell that the Americans after them, likely with Egyptian assistance, were even, then, in the process of plugging all conventional exits from the country.

"I got into Egypt without the Egyptians knowing it," Dilah said, perhaps thinking Ken needed a bit of verbal reassurance. "I doubt it's going to be all that difficult to arrange my exit, and include yours along with it."

"I hope that's the case," Ken said, scooting farther down in his seat, pulling his coat tighter around him.

Their immediate destination turned out to be a small cave in one desert embankment, reached by scrambling over loose stone, in the dark, after the Land Rover, empty of gas, was ditched in a gully and covered with dried brush conveniently (and purposefully?) available for the camouflage.

"Don't tell me," Ken said, when the light of a Coleman lamp revealed cave walls covered in hieroglyphics faded with age. "You've brought me to yet another tomb!"

Dilah laughed. "Pre-dynastic, I believe. Anyway, that's what someone once told me who purported to know such things."

If Ken was curious as to her information source, he didn't press for specifics, and Dilah didn't volunteer any. However, she did oblige by offering him a bit more information about where they were.

"At one time, you know, there was far more rain here than there is now. Settlements extended outward from the Nile as well as running parallel to it."

"Fancy that," Ken said. He wasn't as much interested in Egypt as he was in how they were going to get out of it. Dilah sensed his disinterest and moved to a subject she assumed, correctly, he'd find of more interest.

"There are a couple of sleeping bags over there," she said. "We have our choice of zipping them together, for mutual warmth, or …"

"Yeah, let's zip them together," Ken said, "for mutual warmth."

"You zip them," Dilah said, kneeling by a cache of supplies stacked along one wall. "I'll see if I can drum up a little something to eat before bedtime."

"It's a deal," Ken said.

He located the bags with no difficulty and unrolled each of them. By the time he had their material shaken, aired out, and re-combined into a convenient cloth pocket for two, Dilah had dried fruit and nuts available for dining.

"Nothing fancy," she said, tossing Ken his bags and preparing to open hers, "but, it'll keep the hunger pangs at bay until we can get better."

Actually, at least as far as Ken was concerned, the combination of fruit and nuts tasted damned good. So did the lukewarm water from one of several available canteens.

When the makeshift meal was over, Dilah and Ken both prepared to undress.

"I'm going to leave the lamp on for a bit," she said, "because I want to see if your body is as good as I remember it."

He smiled in a way that might easily have been mistaken for embarrassment by anyone who knew him less well than she did. She was no longer fooled, as she, and most everyone else, at first, was, by his innocent good looks that came across, now, no less innocent with a day's-growth of man-beard on his well-tanned cheeks and chin. She had seen another woman mistake

him for less the trained agent that he was. At the time, Dilah had been thankful he hadn't been out to charm information out of her. By now, she knew full well that he used his attractiveness and physical appeal as expertly as any woman, Dilah included, ever had or did.

"Well?" he asked, fully nude on top of the united sleeping bags.

"At your age, you should be falling apart," she said, making it sound the compliment it was. She had waited until he was completely stripped before finishing her own undress. "I thought for sure you'd have a flabby belly and a limp prick by now."

"Must be the active life I lead," he said and found great comfort in the goose-down cocoon he entered, really looking forward to the additional warmth he'd soon find provided by the woman beside him.

It had been a long time since they'd had sex together. Before, they'd been good together. Very good. Anyway, that's the way he remembered it, and he doubted he remembered it wrong. As many people as he'd fucked in his lifetime, and there had been more than a few, he could still remember the good ones. It was very seldom, however, there were chances for repeats.

"Your nipples are hard," he told her, fascinated by her dark areola puckered from the fullness of her creamy breasts.

"It's the goddamned cold," she said and recognized her luck in having Ken Mal once again on her side of a battle. She recognized her luck, too, in nothing in the interim, between their last meeting and now, having spoiled them on each other. That wasn't always the case with men and women in their business, especially when Ken's participation in the freelance Grey Zone area could so easily have seen him tainted by having previously teamed with some man or woman whose ideologies were radically, and thereby unacceptably, opposed to those of Dilah and Mother Russia. If the Americans hadn't been so kill-happy, she might not have had this moment. If she never had any other reason to thank those bastard Yanks, this would be reason enough.

Their sex was just as good as he remembered. It was just as good as she remembered. It was so good that they milked it for all it was worth. After all, who knew how long it might be, if ever, before circumstances made such intimacy between them again impossible?

CHAPTER TEN

IT WAS A LONG SHOT, but there were factors which pointed toward a very slight possibility of it proving productive. However, considering everything Ken *hadn't been* able to come up with in Rome, thus far, if this last lead didn't pan out, either, it would have to be on to Amsterdam to try Dilah and his luck there.

He was tailing Leonardo Bottocci, because the kid was gay. Denver Rheingold was, or had been, gay. Giovani Corso had been gay. Although that sameness, in itself, was a tenuous basis for linking the three, Ken hoped Bottocci might give him information about Corso or Rheingold, which might, in turn, lead to Rheingold, or to what was left of him.

It would have been infinitely better, and certainly more to the point, to talk to Corso, except the kid was dead. That he died in Luna Park within the same timeframe that had seen Rheingold turn up missing in the same city was what had Ken grasping at Bottocci as a possible "straw".

There were, of course, other contributing factors. Firstly, Rheingold frequently participated in the activities ongoing after dark at Luna Park whenever he was in the city. Secondly, if Rheingold hadn't been in Luna Park the evening the Corso kid died there, Ken found no evidence he'd been anywhere else, either. Thirdly, even if there was no connection between Rheingold, Corso, and Bottocci, there was still the outside chance that the latter—who was a long-time regular at Luna Park— might have, on his very own, run into Rheingold. If Rheingold

had disappeared without any help from the Americans, there was the possibility he had done so by advantaging one or more of his tricks (Corso? Bottocci?), picked up during his late-night Roman trysts. Ken had covered Rheingold's "regular" local playmates well enough to be assured none of them presently helped Rheingold remain incognito. Rheingold had very few males, young or otherwise, who were steadies in his life. Like most of the people in his particular area of expertise, he was inclined to move from person to person to person, rather than settle on just one, as far as his sexual and social lives were concerned.

Other people, not agents within the Grey Area, were less careful. Bottocci had been so close to Corso that their relationship came out in the investigation which followed the latter's brutal murder, and Bottocci had been discharged from the Army as an indirect result. He was now employed as a car mechanic in a garage on the Via Magenta, not far from where he'd taken a small apartment.

Ken chose not to hook up with the ex-soldier at the kid's place. There was no less likely way of getting information than by banging on someone's door and firing off direct questions. The kid was probably already paranoid because of all the trouble caused by his relationship with a fellow soldier.

Not that Ken discarded the possibility of a more direct approach. If his more subtle means of cross-examination failed, turning up nothing where there appeared even a hint of something, he was prepared to get what he wanted, no matter how it was necessary.

This particular night, Bottocci had taken to the streets shortly after dark, wearing—Ken noted—an Army uniform, despite the kid and the Army having parted company. Ken correctly suspected Bottocci's fondness for his old uniform had little to do with anything except that it remained an excellent card to be played in any game of hustling Roman walkways and shadows. Anyone spotted in uniform in Luna Park was immediately identified, rightly or wrongly, as a soldier looking for extra cash to

supplement a paltry Army income. It was seldom that anyone in uniform in the park didn't charge for fun and games.

Bottocci took a bus from his apartment to the Monument Victor Emmanuel II, that wedding-cake architectural monstrosity that dominated the Roman skyline, and he walked the Via dei Fori Imperiali toward the Coliseum, the latter already lit at its end of the roadway. Ken, who had followed the bus in his rented car, pulled ahead of the walking youth, while keeping Bottocci in sight in the rearview mirror. He parked on the opposite side of the street, near the juncture of the Imperiali with the Piazza del Colosseo and got out of his car only when Bottocci passed him by. From there, he followed, on foot, moving in closer when the young man reached one of the stairways to park level. Ken had no intention of losing him once the lights of the roadway surrendered to the shadows of the ruins and shrubbery.

The two weren't alone as, first, Bottocci, then, Ken, topped the stairway. Already, there were the lookers and the looked-at making their rounds, spotting potential. Sexual acts were already ongoing in the bushes, behind ruins, and amidst trees.

Ken didn't wait long; firstly, the area was darker than he thought it would be; secondly, he didn't want to lose Bottocci to someone else. He moved in close enough, fast enough, to make it appear as if he was preparing to make a serious proposition, but he aborted before completion. He made himself look interested but nervous. Bottocci would hopefully see that as a sign of someone out to make contact but too embarrassed, or made too ill at ease by the surroundings, to take the initiative. As Ken wore an expensive Brioni suit, his air of embarrassed innocence was enough to make Bottocci figure it to his benefit to move in on an obviously interested paycheck before someone else beat him to it.

By that point, the kid could hardly believe there was someone as good looking as Ken patrolling the park, or that Ken had so quickly expressed interest in what the young Italian had to offer.

If the youth, and any of the others, like him, who roamed the premises that night, remembered that it hadn't been all that

long since someone had killed Giovani Corso, there, in similar darkness, such negative thoughts, and accompanying fears, were thrust aside. Life went on. Luna Park was too well known for the type of services it provided after nightfall, and, thereby, too convenient to be abandoned for some less-known location. Besides, if there was a killer on the prowl, he'd find his next victim, no matter the darkness of *any* street, park, or alleyway into which a hustler might try to escape. Further rationalization for continued use of the park was how there had been no immediate follow-up murder or murders. This insinuated Corso had been killed by someone merely dissatisfied with the kid's sexual services. Crimes of passion were very seldom repeated. After all, passion, as any hustler could tell you, was short-lived.

"You a tourist?" Leonardo asked, having approached Ken at one of the decapitated columns that fronted the section of ruins looking directly out over the lighted Coliseum.

"Pardon?" Ken asked, continuing his ill-at-ease act.

"A tourist?" Leonardo repeated, more impressed by Ken's good looks now that he saw them more up-close. "All that blond hair, you know?" he said with a wide smile. "It doesn't look Italian."

"Oh," Ken said. In a move that seemed self-conscious, but wasn't, his right hand ran through his short-cropped, silky strands. "Yeah, I'm a tourist, for sure."

"American?" Leonardo asked. He pegged Ken as American, despite the expensive Italian suit. That the two conversed in English seemed to confirm.

"Yeah, American," Ken said and sounded nervous. There was no need to go into details regarding his real nationality which he sometimes even forgot. American was good enough for the present scenario, and Ken's English was certainly good enough to pass close scrutiny from any expert; an expert Bottocci was not.

"Enjoying Roman night life?" the young hustler asked; he wanted this handsome blond American, verified by the decided stirring of Leonardo's cock. There was something he found

appealing about Ken so obviously coming across as guilty as all hell in just being there, doing what he was doing. It gave Leonardo suspicion that Ken didn't do this sort of thing very often. Shit, maybe the American was married and wondering what in the hell he was doing with a handsome young Italian man when he had American-wife's tight pussy awaiting him back in his hotel room.

"Yeah, nice," Ken said. "Rome, I mean."

"You should see more of it and more of us Romans, you know?" Leonardo suggested; his sentence was rife with double-entendre. "The city isn't just old ruins and fancy hotels?"

Ken knew the truth of that, all right. Also, he knew he had hooked his 'fish,' and now just had to play him a little bit before reeling him in.

"It's not easy," Ken said. "Meeting locals, I mean."

"I'm a local," Leonardo reminded, extending his right hand. "Leonardo is my name; I'm glad to make your acquaintance."

Ken took the young man's hand that delivered a persistent squeeze that didn't allow Ken's fingers a quick withdrawal.

"My name is Ken," Ken said. There was little need to lie, as long as they kept on a purely first-name basis. Hustler-customer relationships weren't known for in-depth explorations of personal backgrounds.

"Hello, then, Ken," Leonardo said. He'd made no effort to be free of Ken's hand quite yet.

"You're in the military?" Ken asked, figuring the question couldn't be considered out of bounds, since the kid's uniform made Bottocci's supposed occupation obvious. The question, Ken knew, also, laid wide open Bottocci's spiel about low salaries in the Army. Ken was anxious to move this right along, and nothing would do that faster than getting the nitty-gritty money issue quickly out of the way.

Bottocci jumped at the offered lead.

"The Army doesn't pay much," he said, reluctantly, releasing Ken's hand. In a well-practiced, seemingly unaffected move-ment of his right hand, he adjusted the evident swelling of hard

dick at his crotch. "I came down here, tonight, to see if I could earn a few extra bucks, maybe. You know what I mean?"

Ken managed to look so additionally embarrassed and ill at ease that it came across even in the darkness.

"I imagine, though, that a handsome American like you doesn't have to pay for his amusements," Leonardo said. "Too bad, I say, for the both of us."

Ken looked this way, and, then, that. He was aware of shadows moving all around, some watching, but most just intent upon making contacts of their own for the evening.

"If you should ever think you wouldn't mind paying, though, be sure to look me up, first thing," Leonardo said, suspecting he was going to get everything he wanted this evening: a hand-some blond American, some American dollars, and, maybe, even a big tip as well. "I can do just about anything you might like. You know? Man, I mean, *anything*. You aren't going to find anyone, anywhere, as good at all the right things as I am."

Ken swallowed hard, stuffing his hands deep into his pants pockets. He did his country-bumpkin routine that managed to look genuine even when performed within his twelve-hundred dollar suit.

"How much?" Ken asked uneasily.

Leonardo told him, actually lowering his going price, because he didn't want to lose this one. It wasn't very often Leonardo ran across someone he wanted more than money, but he sure as hell wanted this blond American.

"And, you'll do *anything?*" Ken ventured tentatively.

"As long as it isn't too kinky," Leonardo qualified. He couldn't imagine anyone as clean-cut as Ken being too deeply into things too far beyond the realm of possibility.

"I'd kind of like to…," Ken began, and, then, hesitated, as if it really was a little hard to get it out.

"Like to do what, stud?" Leonardo encouraged, smiling widely, knowing he was home free. "I'll bet you are a *stud,* too, aren't you? I'll bet you fuck the girls and make them go ape-shit, don't you? Want to fuck me, and make me go ape-shit? Huh?

Want me to let you deep-fuck my man-pussy?"

"Jesus!" Ken said, shuffling back and forth, as if someone had caught him playing pocket-pool.

"If that's what you want, buddy, that's what you can have," Leonardo promised. "For the going price, there isn't anyone around here with a tight asshole that can please you more than mine can."

CHAPTER ELEVEN

"JESUS! JESUS! JESUS!" Jerry Crowlson said, put down the receiver of the phone, and glanced around the small office assigned him in the U.S. Embassy, London.

He should have known there would be a fuck-up. Why was there always a fuck-up? Couldn't there be just one time when someone could tell him not to worry, that things would be taken care of, and things were taken care of? Nothing sure as hell was taken care of, this time! Not according to the scenario he'd been led to expect.

He flipped through the telephone directory at one corner of his desk and came up with a number.

"Eldridge Filholden, please," he said, after he'd dialed and the phone was engaged at the other end.

"Who shall I say is calling?" the voice asked. It was a man's voice with little inflection. Jerry might just as well have been talking to some goddamned robot and possibly was.

Hell, he wished he *were,* convinced he could get faster and better results from some mechanical marvel than from so many incompetent human beings who tried to pass themselves off as experts in their fields.

"This is Jerry Crowlson, CIA, wanting to speak with Filholden," Jerry said. "Be kind enough to tell him that I'm not about to take no for an answer."

"Hold the line, please," the voice said. Again, no emotion, as if the owner was used to receiving calls from people making demands.

Jerry, though wasn't *just* making demands. He had every intention of speaking to Eldridge and damned fast. And if Eldridge couldn't come up with some answers, good and quick, Jerry had every intention of finding someone who could.

Goddamn, Eldridge was a fuck-up! Jerry was furious that he'd had to verify that on his own. By all rights, Eldridge should have been on the line the minute it was obvious the Egyptian thing was queered. For Christ's sake, Jerry was up to this thing to his neck, and....

"Jerry, this is Eldridge," the familiar voice said into Jerry's right ear.

"Well, Eldridge," Jerry said, hardly able to control his fury, "I suggest you get your ass over here right away before I start moaning long and loud about how much your Egyptian caper went so fucking awry."

He hung up with a bang, hoping to jolt some goddamned sense into that jackass on the other end of the line.

He half expected Eldridge to call right back. It would have been just like that asshole to come on indignant as all hell, asking Jerry for some kind of explanation, as if Jerry was the one at fault. The bastard was just the kind of prick to try and bluff his way out of this. Well, Jerry wasn't having any goddamned bluffing.

When the phone didn't immediately ring, Jerry told himself that Eldridge was possibly simply going to ignore him.

"Ignore me, and that'll be one very bad career move, you shit!" Jerry warned. He'd give the incompetent turd fifteen minutes, and, then, just watch the shit hit the fan.

Eldridge was there in ten, which, more than anything, should have told Jerry the call had been taken quite seriously, although Eldridge made every initial effort to feign ignorance of what could possibly have Jerry so upset.

"Now, what is this *really* all about?" Eldridge asked. His stance was that of a superior officer who, only the result of his good graces, had decided to humor a subordinate's outburst. In fact, by any chain of command, there was no way Jerry should

have successfully summoned Eldridge, instead of vice versa.

"I suppose you weren't even going to tell me that he's in Rome," Jerry said, standing and dropping a clenched fist to the top of the desk with a resounding thud.

"Who?" Eldridge asked.

"Ken Mal!" Jerry said, and he could tell just by the expression on Eldridge's face that the man hadn't had a clue.

The bastard actually hadn't known!

"Jesus H. Christ!" Jerry said, sitting down. "I don't believe this is happening. Did you, or did you not tell me that you were seeing to Mal's termination through Glenn Jargreave in Egypt?"

"There may have been unforeseen problems," Eldridge ventured, at a loss as to what else to say. Obviously, he'd been caught with his pants down, not the faintest notion how he was going to get them pulled up again without getting fucked royally. Not only was it bad enough that Mal had slipped out of Egypt, undetected, despite the complex network of snares set out to keep him from doing just that, but Eldridge had to find out from the goddamned CIA.

"I suppose you were just going to sit around and wait for the bastard to reach London and pick me off like a sitting duck," Jerry said. It wasn't a question.

"It's hardly likely you're in any present or immediate danger," Eldridge said, still trying to cover his butt.

"You and your man botched Mal's termination, and you don't think Mal is going to suspect the attempt didn't somehow include me? Who sent him to Egypt in the first place? Who gave him Glenn Jargreave's name as contact? What in the hell...are you...a fucking idiot?"

In truth, Eldridge didn't know what had happened. More than anyone, he'd give his eyeteeth to find out.

"Why don't you tell me what you think Mal is presently doing in Rome?" Eldridge suggested, making a feeble attempt to get a little more of the control back in his possession.

"You're not even going to pretend he's already dead?" Jerry ventured with icy sarcasm. "Or, maybe you'd like to assure me

that he's still in Egypt?"

"Quite frankly, we're not sure where he is at the moment," Eldridge admitted. It was a confession he wouldn't have made, except that, by that point, it was superfluous.

"He's in Rome, goddamn it!" Jerry shouted. "In bloody Rome!"

"Says who?" Eldridge asked, desperately trying to maintain some semblance of calm. Goddamn, there were heads that would roll for this humiliating cock-up. He just hoped one of them wasn't his.

"One of *my CIA* informants says, that's who!" Jerry said facetiously. "Thank God, the disappearance of Candle, Rheingold, and Darnel didn't leave my organization completely without assets as regards the Grey Zone."

"May I use your telephone?" Eldridge asked. "It's really quite an important call."

Jerry didn't give him permission, but Eldridge used the telephone anyway."

CHAPTER TWELVE

LEONARDO BOTTOCCI EYED his flushed face, tousled black hair, and attractively dilated black eyes in the mirror. He turned out the bathroom light and crossed the threshold into the adjoining bedroom.

Ken Mal was propped up on the bed, the sheet dropped so that his muscled chest was uncovered. Leonardo once again thanked his lucky stars for this particular evening and went to join Ken on the bed.

"Was I your first?" Leonardo asked, scooting down beneath the covers, arranging pillows so he could lean, along with Ken, against the headboard.

"First what?" Ken asked, still completely into his role.

"First man you've ever had sex with," Leonardo said.

"Oh," Ken said, appearing as if confused. "No," he said, finally, after a very long pause.

Leonardo was obviously disappointed.

"Don't get me wrong," Ken hurried quickly into the breach. "I don't do this sort of thing all of the time. As a matter of fact, I've only done it once before."

That made Leonardo feel a little better. He didn't know why, but he could get really turned on by seducing straight guys, or guys whose gay experiences were at a bare minimum.

"Actually, at the park, this evening, I was looking for the last kid I tricked with," Ken said. "I thought he was you, as a matter of fact. That's why I came up to you and then backed away so suddenly."

"He was a soldier, too?" asked Leonardo who *had,* after all, been in uniform earlier that evening.

"Yeah, he was," Ken said. "Your uniform was another thing that had me thinking you might be one and the same guy."

"Was he good in bed?" Leonardo asked. Knowing how good a time he had just shown Ken, he was willing to risk a comparison. "Was he better than me?"

"Giovani was damned good," Ken said. "That's for sure. Whether he was better than you, well, that remains to be seen, doesn't it? I mean, the night is still young."

If Ken continued right on with his apparently harmless banter, he had, nonetheless, noticed how Leonardo had reacted to Giovani's name.

"Something wrong?" Ken asked, knowing he was well on his way.

"Wrong?" Leonardo echoed, suddenly very ill at ease. "Why would anything be wrong?"

"Hell, I don't know," Ken said with a shrug. "The way you acted, I thought maybe you and Giovani might be old friends—or rivals—or tricks—or lovers—or something. Did you know him?"

Leonardo tried to take a good look at Ken to reassure this wasn't the same man who had picked Giovani up and went with him into the shadows of Luna Park on that one fateful night. Oh, Ken and the other man were both blonds, but the similarity stopped there, except for both being exceptionally good looking. Leonardo had been cruising the killer, if the other blond *was* the killer, just moments before Giovani had moved in to stake claim.

Leonardo shivered at the memory of how it might well have been him, instead of Giovani, dead that night.

"Are you sure you're okay?" Ken asked. He had expected some reaction, but nothing quite so intense.

"I'm fine!" Leonardo insisted

He wasn't feeling fine at all. Every time he thought about that evening, he ended up feeling ill. Partly, it was because the

police might well have used his description of the likely killer to catch the guy; except, Leonardo hadn't given them a description. He'd panicked when word made the rounds at the barracks that the missing Giovani was found dead in the bushes of Luna Park. Leonardo hadn't been the only one to panic, either. Carlo Gendellinni, likewise out that night to make a few extra bucks, had panicked, too. Everybody knew what could be insinuated by the location of the body. Giovani had been selling himself to queers. Neither Carlo nor Leonardo wanted that stigma attached to them in the investigation which followed, and it would have become attached if ever made common knowledge that they, as well as Giovani, had been in Luna Park that evening. They had, therefore, protected each other by giving each other an alibi to put them, together, elsewhere at the time. In the end, though, not even their alibis protected them completely from the scandal. Giovani, it seems, had fucked and sucked just about every one of his fellow soldiers, or been fucked and sucked by them; it hadn't taken long for *that* to get out. Oh, there never had been any real proof that Giovani and Leonardo had had sex together in the shower room (where they had), but the whispers resulting from the police inquiry were enough so that Leonardo decided to accept the offered early discharge. He was, after all, as guilty as sin.

After he was out of the service, he'd thought, on several different occasions, that he'd go back to the cops to tell them about the blond man. By that time, however, he was convinced his meager description wouldn't help anybody find anybody. Besides, he found a good job at the garage, and nobody there knew he was in anyway connected with the murdered queer. Everyone at the garage thought Leonardo had honorably fulfilled his full term of military service before discharge.

"Leonardo?" Ken asked. "You look a little pale."

"I'm fine," Leonardo insisted, shaking his head to clear it. He'd be fine once he got all that crap about Giovani buried deeply away, inside of him, where it should be.

"You knew Giovani, right?" Ken asked, figuring to strike

while the proverbial iron was hot. "Damn, you did, didn't you?"

"Yeah, I knew him!" Leonardo admitted, albeit reluctantly, wishing to hell the subject had never come up, wondering why and how it had. "I knew him, and let's leave it to hell like that, please. I don't fucking want to talk about him! Okay?"

Ken gave the impression of someone taken back just a little by Leonardo's attitude. He was so successful in looking bewildered that he immediately had Leonardo feeling a little ridiculous.

"Look, my handsome blond American new-found friend," Leonardo said, figuring he might very well owe Ken some kind of explanation. "This Giovani you're talking about, well, you see, he's dead."

"Dead?" Ken responded with all the surprise he could muster under the circumstances.

"Yeah, dead," Leonardo verified. "And, I'd just as soon not talk about it. You know?"

"Sometimes talking helps," Ken persisted.

"Yeah? Sometimes not," Leonardo assured.

"Come on, I really want to know," Ken said. "I really liked the guy. Just how *did* he die?"

"Goddamn it, I said I don't want to talk about it!" Leonardo said loudly. "Do you have to be fucking hit over the head with a hammer, or can you just take the hint?"

He did end up talking about it, of course. And after Ken had gotten it all out of him, Leonardo could only wish that he'd been a little less reluctant to part with the information in the first place.

CHAPTER THIRTEEN

"I GUESS THAT ONLY LEAVES Paris or Amsterdam, right?" Dilah asked, eyeing Ken over the edge of her glass. She was drinking white wine. When on assignment, she drank nothing stronger, and she seldom had more than a small glass of that at any one time.

"I think that's a safe assumption," Ken agreed. "From Leonardo Bottocci's description of the guy with whom Giovani trotted off into the dingle berries that night, I'd venture odds that it *was* Denver Rheingold. Since nothing in Rheingold's background indicates he ever killed any of his tricks, before, though, I think the blame for Giovani Corso's murder can safely be placed on someone else's doorstep, even though no one seems to have seen Rheingold since the night the Corso kid was deep-sixed."

"Have you any feedback from your Grey Zone queries regarding Johan Darnel?" Dilah asked. Her pulse began to quicken. It always did when she thought she might be closing in on her objective.

"I'd say the chances were good he was on that train to Amsterdam," Ken said. "He went there regularly and was due for a return."

"Business?" Dilah ventured. Her own contacts were able to come up with very little concerning the shadowy Johan Darnel. Therefore, she was still counting upon Ken's contacts within the Grey Zone to be more informative. If they weren't, Dilah saw little chance of locating the missing agent.

"Actually, his trips were usually for pleasure," Ken said, pacing the room. After what had happened between Leonardo Bottocci and Ken, Ken was anxious to get out of Rome. It wasn't the gayness of the encounter that bothered him. In his line of business, he'd bedded all kinds to get information. There had been, though, something about the scene he'd enacted with Leonardo that had been especially disturbing, as if the pleasure he got from beating information out of the young man was somehow directly connected to the pleasure he got from fucking Leonardo afterwards. If there was any correlation, it hinted a side of Ken to which he would just as soon not have been introduced.

He shook his head to clear it, accounting his disconcertion to what he expected might await him in Amsterdam. If Ken had only vague imaginings of what sado-masochism might suddenly hold out for him, by way of some kind of perverse fascination, he'd recently unearthed a helluva lot of deep-seated whispers regarding Johan Darnel's genuine penchant for whips and chains.

CHAPTER FOURTEEN

"WELL, WHAT DO YOU THINK?" Ken asked. "Can it be done?"

Brandon Thompson sat in the armchair across from him. Anyway, that was the name the man used that week. In the past, he'd been David Torn, Samuel Peaks, and Reginald Wilson.

Brandon, like Ken, was a member of the clandestine free-lance Grey-Zone fraternity. Rumor had it that he was Greek. He looked Greek, which meant he might just as likely be Swedish. He had curly black hair, large black eyes, a nose that looked as if it had been broken once too often, and lips that were decidedly too thin for his accompanying blockish facial contours.

Ken had utilized his services on several occasions. He trusted him about as much as anyone within the always shifting loyalties of the Grey-Zone arena.

"*Anything,* I suppose, can be arranged for the right price," Brandon replied, smoking a cigarette that trailed spirals of smelly smoke to form a blue cloud along the ceiling. "That's what you were assuming, were you not?"

He smiled. Ken tossed him a bankbook which the man skillfully caught in his free hand and opened. He whistled upon seeing the balance inside.

"If necessary, there's more where that came from," Ken said.

"I think this might be adequate," Brandon said, depositing the book in the pocket of his flannel shirt. The shirt was open halfway down its front, revealing a section of barrel chest matted with thick black hair and hung with eleven gold chains

aligned with myriad assorted gold attachments.

"*Not* a termination," Ken emphasized.

"Of course not," Brandon agreed with a widening smile that revealed evidence that all of his gold wasn't strung around his neck. "It's not very often that I come across such a reward for just *setting up* a termination."

"The man set me up for a kill that failed," Ken said. "Failed, I might add, through no fault of his."

Brandon shrugged, giving all impression that, while he'd insinuated a bit of interest as to what might lie behind their arrangement, he really wasn't interested at all.

"It's the nature of the game we're in that we kill, and that people often try to kill us, in return," he did say. "In this ever-changing environment, though, this guy might well turn out to be on your side tomorrow, yes?"

"The sooner all members at the playing board realize there's not now, nor has there ever been, free hunting season on this particular piece of the game, the safer I'm going to feel. I want the next guy who comes after me to think very carefully about what happened to those who tried before him. I'm not a pawn to be moved at will or sacrificed at the whim of some other player."

"You say he's in London?" Brandon asked, granting Ken the point just taken.

* * * * * * *

ACTUALLY, THE SUBJECT of their discussion, Eldridge Filholden, as well as his CIA counterpart, Jerry Crowlson, were in Rome. Considering it was Jerry's CIA contacts who had uncovered Ken Mal's exit from Cairo and arrival in Rome, it had been decided that Jerry should finally be brought fully into the loop that involved the search for the three missing Grey Area agents. Oh, Jerry had received peripheral informa-tion before, when Eldridge had informed him how the CIA, having brought Ken Mal into the picture, had interfered with the special-ops project in operation, but Jerry had never been

totally briefed—until now. The sudden expansion to include him within the *need-to-know* circle was primarily the result of his CIA information sources proving of more worth than anyone at the disposal of the special-projects unit. It was important that Ken Mal be found before he located any of the missing agents, especially since Jerry's most recent reports on Ken's activities now hinted at possible Russian involvement.

"Mal could have been of tremendous help in all of this," Jerry said at the conclusion of his briefing. "Tremendous help," he repeated in emphasis. "If most information lines with the freelance Grey Area are closed to us, now, he still has access to them."

"Yes, well...," Powlin Cheney, Eldridge Filholden's immediate superior, said from his position at head of the table. He coughed and fidgeted in his chair in obvious indication that he followed Jerry's reasoning—if only in retrospect.

"It simply would have been too risky to allow Mal to stumble onto what was happening!" Eldridge chimed in. If Powlin chose to forget the reasoning behind Ken Mal's proposed termination, Eldridge certainly didn't. "Mal shifts sides, as does most of his Grey-Zone ilk, like a goddamned ping-pong ball. We would have had no guarantees, whatsoever, that his success would have seen benefits actually coming to us and not to someone offering him a higher wage, like the Russians. Surely, we all see that."

"What *I* see," Jerry emphasized, "is that a man previously on our side is presently on the other side, not because someone enticed him there with offers of greater financial rewards, at least not at the beginning, but because of your unsuccessfully orchestrated attempt to kill him."

"It was too dangerous to allow even the *possibility* of any of this getting into the hands of someone who couldn't be trusted not to turn it over to the Russians, the Chinese, or to whomever else would come rushing into the breach with money bags full and drawstrings wide open," Eldridge insisted.

"Better *we* have had him on even a tentative leash than the

Russians who probably have him now! " Jerry said, getting more than a small amount of pleasure in sticking that point home. He did not like Eldridge. He did not like Powlin. Certainly, he didn't like the way they and their special-ops group had somehow been conjured by God-only-knew what high echelon to infringe upon an area of influence that obviously was better handled by the CIA. Why in the hell couldn't those ignorant bastards, in the chain of command "upstairs," realize the CIA as the superior organization that it was and quit their constant tinkering to come up with something they always figured better but never was? In fact, it almost always happened that those "somethings better" turned out to be "somethings worse." The present special group involved in all of this, Eldridge and Powlin included, was just another prime case in point.

"It's pure conjecture, at this juncture, that the Russians have reeled in Mal!" Eldridge reminded, feeling very much as if he carried, entirely on his back, the reputation of his side. Powlin sat there as if he well realized his people had been *wrong*—(READ THAT: *Eldridge Filholden had been wrong*)—in arranging a termination which had since come to endanger the project even more than it had been endangered in the first place.

"The ease with which Mal exited Egypt would certainly hint to his having had an assist from someone?" Jerry reminded. Having that verbal knife thrust into place, he now twisted it with relish. "My CIA reports hint of a prominent Russian agent, a woman, in Egypt, at one and the same time as Mal, and now sighted, here, in Rome, where Mal, too, has been sighted. A coincidence, gentlemen?"

"I think, perhaps, we've lost track of the purpose behind this little get-together," Powlin said, finally, deciding there was little to be gained in letting the heated discussion continue along its present lines. If he had to admit that Jerry was right in his assessment of the bungling so far, that bungling did reflect back upon Powlin, as head of the special-ops group involved, even if Powlin could point an accusing finger at Eldridge. After all, Eldridge was no more or less than a Powlin subordinate.

And while little failures along the way could be foisted off on a subordinate's shoulders (Powlin not all sure this failure had been a *small* one), the ultimate collapse of the project was going to bring the bricks right down around Powlin's ears. "We're not here to discuss what has come before, except as it might help us prevent future screws-up. I'm certainly prepared to concede that mistakes have been made."

Eldridge frowned in disapproval.

"Now, what I would really like for us to do, gentlemen," Powlin continued, "seeing as how the excellent facilities of the special projects group has now been fortunate enough to be supplemented by those facilities available through Mr. Crowlson of the CIA, is to...."

* * * * * * *

IN ROOM 211 of the Hotel de l'Europe, overlooking the Amstel where that river meets Singel Canal in the center of Amsterdam, Ken Mal picked up the telephone, and, when the caller asked for Brandon Thompson, handed it over. Brandon spoke only briefly before stretching to return the receiver to its hook.

"It sounds as if we might have a lead regarding the missing Johan Darnel," Brandon said, leaning to stub the remains of his cigarette into a nearby ashtray. "I'm informed he's known to frequent a certain number fifty-five Kalorstraat in the red-light district of this fair city. A lady of the evening; a very *special* lady of the evening...."

Ken caught the intended insinuation.

"...by the name of Heidi Tenkaarn. Would you like me personally to check this out?"

"Why don't you concern yourself with our other project?" Ken suggested. "I'll look into the possible involvement of Miss Tenkaarn."

"As you wish," Brandon conceded, tried to keep the smile off his face but didn't succeed.

"My visit to the woman will be purely business, I assure

you!" Ken insisted, imagining what prurient thoughts were presently crossing his associate's mind to cause that man's obvious amusement.

Despite his pointed protest, Ken *was* getting an erection.

CHAPTER FIFTEEN

"ANY IDEA WHAT THIS meet-up is for?" Eldridge Filholden asked, knowing—even before his question was out of his mouth—it was the very last thing he should put to his distraught boss.

"And, why, I wonder, was I hoping that maybe *you* could tell me what it's all about?" Powlin Cheney replied. "After all, we only brought Crowlson and the CIA in on this, didn't turn it over to them, whole hog, did we? Or, did I miss out on something somewhere along the line?"

Jerry arrived with a smug look that had Powlin and Eldridge steeled for the worst. Where they had been trying futilely to come up with a clue as to where Ken Mal had disappeared within the maze of Roman buildings and streets, coming up with a big fat goose egg, it seemed more than apparent that Jerry had been a little more successful. Though, not for a moment did Eldridge believe Jerry was giving full cooperation. Oh, no! Eldridge saw right through that sonofabitch. Jerry Crowlson, still ticked off about having so long been kept out of the loop, regarding the specifics of the project, was now prepared to make everybody involved before his involvement look like an ass.

Powlin gave a scowl that more than relayed the same frustrations as those of his subordinate, and Eldridge couldn't very well blame him. Powlin came out no less a fool, in all of this than Eldridge, and, since policy decisions theoretically stopped at Powlin, he likely appeared an even bigger incompetent.

"We have something," Jerry said, standing at the table,

his fingers pressed tightly against its top. "I figured you'd be anxious for me to share and let you give a hand in the analysis."

"Most anxious," Powlin said, his eyes shooting daggers at Eldridge who successfully avoided eye contact.

"First off," Jerry said, enjoying every minute; although it had meant busting his butt, to the detriment of other CIA work projects with which he was involved, "it might have helped tremendously if one of you had let me know that Denver Rheingold was a practicing gay."

Powlin's mouth dropped. "A faggot?" he managed finally.

"So, what if he was?" Eldridge jumped in, well aware shit was going to hit the fan if Jerry somehow proved that unmentioned factor had something to do with anything.

The problem for Eldridge, and everyone else, of course, was always getting any kind of viable information on any of the agents who operated freelance within the Grey Zone. Hell, those bastards went through so many name changes, nationality changes, physical changes, and personality changes, by the time they arrived on any scene, it was difficult separating fact from fiction from conjecture. Now, that the subject had been brought up, Eldridge could remember having sometime, somewhere, read a "supposition" that Rheingold might—just *might*—have homosexual leanings. Even if true, though, one or two romps with another hard dick in the hay didn't mean a full-fledged entre into Queerdom was the result.

"We're talking as queer as a three-dollar bill," Jerry said, thoroughly enjoying the expression on the faces of these special-projects bigwigs who apparently couldn't even find their assholes to wipe without assistance. "One of his favorite haunts for contacting fellow queers was in Luna Park, which is a stretch of walkway, ruins, and shrubbery directly across from the Coliseum."

"We're familiar with Luna Park and what goes on there!" Powlin snapped. This was a lie, at least as far as Denver Rheingold ever being there was concerned.

"Do get on and quit sadistically dragging it all out!" Eldridge

insisted. At the same time, he realized that statement didn't likely endear him any the more to Jerry who already likely hated Eldridge's guts. Had Eldridge used better judgment, he would have swallowed all of his goddamned pride and tried to maneuver Jerry into willingly giving the CIA's helping hand so obviously needed to get them all out of this present mess, instead of providing Jerry every incentive to pound a few more nails, even more tightly, into the descended lid of Eldridge's coffin.

"During that very fuzzy period between Rheingold last being seen alive, and his turning up missing, there seems to have been a murder in Luna Park of a young man named Giovani Corso."

"Jesus, do get to the point!" Eldridge again insisted. So far, none of this sounded all that pertinent, anyway.

"Giovani Corso had a friend named Leonardo Bottocci," Jerry continued, undaunted.

"Is all of this sordid detail leading somewhere?" Powlin asked knowing—like Eldridge—that he would be far better off courting this man rather than continuing to insinuate that Jerry was some kind of certifiable idiot.

"I don't know if it is or not," Jerry said, "but if it isn't, why don't you tell me why Leonardo Bottocci is, right this minute, in the hospital, probably put there by none other than Ken Mal?"

That shut the bastards up, Jerry thought, trying very hard to keep the satisfied Cheshire-cat grin off his face.

CHAPTER SIXTEEN

SHE WAS PLEASANTLY SURPRISED when he walked up, brazen as you please, and tapped on her window. Oh, she knew she'd smiled at him when he walked by, a few minutes before. She had flicked her big, black bullwhip at him, too, and, then, let its phallic leather length glide sensuously over the inside of one of her naked, creamy thighs, by way of additional come-on. But, hell, she did that to almost every guy who looked her way. She was a businesswoman, for Christ's sake, and had to "whip" up business the best way she knew how.

She figured herself as having wasted her time with him. He looked too squeaky clean. Something about his attractive blond looks just didn't jive with those of her typical customer. Having been in the business as long as she had, having had a whole telephone book of past tricks from which to compile her criterion for her typical john, she still couldn't make this blond, back at her window, fit the stereotypical mold.

However, no denying he went through all of the motions of looking interested, right down to flashing a wad of high-denomination Euros that would choke a horse. She motioned him to the door, unlocking it to let him in.

"You come to share some of your goodness with me, have you?" she asked. She referred not only to his money in his hand but to the hard cock she could now tell he was carrying around in his pants; obviously, he *was* interested.

He smiled. Goddamn, he had pretty teeth! This definitely meant he wasn't English. Dimples, too. All that blond hair. A

body that looked in A-1 shape. Not that she was complaining about any or all of that. Hell, no. She'd be crazy to complain about perfection. He probably had a nice wife at home, whom he loved dearly, but who he came to discover just couldn't give him all that he wanted in the sack. Well, he'd come to the right person and place.

He peeled off several of those big bills he'd been waving at her through the window. He let her see how he added a few extra to what he finally extended in her direction.

"I hear you're the best in your area of expertise," Ken said. "I thought I'd find out whether or not you can give me what I'm specifically after."

"I think you're going to come away damned pleased," she boasted, folding the money and poking it deeply into impressive cleavage provided by the meets-up of her large breasts hoisted by the half-cups of her black-leather brassiere.

She went to the door and locked it, pulling the red curtains to cut off their view from and of the street.

"Come on into the back where we can make ourselves a bit more comfortable," she said and dragged the bullwhip behind her, as if she was a fisherman trolling for marlin.

He followed her into a space defined by more reds curtains. The room was bigger than the one with its display chair facing the window. He sat down on a small stool, deciding the room was no different from other such rooms, except, of course, for the chain apparatus that dangled from the ceiling, and the extensive bondage and discipline equipment probably stored in one or all of the three bureaus against one curtained wall.

"Now, then," she said, striking one of her best poses—hands on hips—and trailing the bullwhip along one of her legs before letting the rope of leather curl snake-like on the floor, "you want to play out some particular fantasy? Or, having admitted my expertise, are you confident enough to let me improvise?"

Ken hadn't made any movement to undress. A lot of men, especially when first confronting her, had to be coaxed into loosening up. This, she recognized as merely the feeling-out

period necessary for each participant to become accustomed to the other. By the time this one became a regular, he and she would have his needs down so pat that there would never again be even a trace of the presently existing uneasiness.

"You think you know what I want?" Ken asked, wondering if he was really turned on by this woman all done up in leather. Admittedly, there was a certain something he found sexually stimulating about it, but he wasn't there to fulfill any of his conscious or unconscious fantasies, no matter the illusion he presented.

"What *do* you want, honey?" she asked, her posturing giving all indication that if anyone could provide it, she could.

"I want you to tell me all you know about Johan Darnel," he said. "I'm especially anxious to find out where he's managed to hide away as of late."

"Johan who?" she asked. If Ken didn't known better, he would have thought she wasn't even vaguely familiar with the name. He did, though, know better. His source was impeccable, and this was definitely where he'd been sent.

"Maybe this will refresh your memory," he said, reaching into an inside coat pocket and producing a photograph. Admittedly, it wasn't a very good one; no agent ever, knowingly, willingly, allowed visuals to be taken, but Dilah had provided the picture, gotten from somewhere, and it was good enough so that someone familiar with the subject would be able to identify him.

If her memory was jolted, her expression didn't show it. She handed the picture back. Her previous willingness-to-please façade was suddenly jettisoned. She'd known damned good and well that this stud was too good to be true.

"Who, or what, in the hell are you?" she asked. "A cop?"

He shook his head.

"A private dick?"

"Merely a man who wants to locate Johan Darnel," Ken said, "and who thinks you can help."

"Well, I've never set eyes on the guy in that picture," she insisted, already planning how she would maneuver out of this.

If he'd asked for just about anything else, especially sexually, she could and would likely have given it to him, in spades. But he had to go and spoil everything by asking about Johan Darnel. She wouldn't give him that information. He likely wouldn't believe her, even if she did.

"You'll save us a helluva lot of time, effort, and bother, by telling me what you know, now," Ken said, his voice taking on an obvious edge of nastiness.

She was no Little Miss Innocent, confronted for the first time by an obnoxious bully. She was a street-wise lady who knew just how she was going to handle this and the shit he was suddenly dealing. She had two alternatives. If the one didn't work, she'd call upon the other. Either way, this bastard was going to be one sorry sonofabitch in having ever started up with her.

Alternative one, however, was quickly taken out of play, literally, by Ken coming quickly forward, taking hold of her whip, and giving it the forceful tug that ripped it free of her grip.

"Max!" she shouted, having quickly realized that she dealt with someone possibly as street-wise as she was, no matter how fresh from the farm he looked.

Trained to keep quiet and out of the way…trained, also, to come on call…her Rottweiler hadn't been caught napping. Max exited his living space, behind one curtain, and made an immediate beeline for Ken.

The dog, though, was no more successful at removing Ken, as a threat, than the whip had been. The knife Ken reflexively drew penetrated the animal's neck, and, simultaneously, diverted the canine's angle of attack to shift its forward momentum and bang the resulting fatally wounded carcass hard against one red-curtained wall.

"Sweet Jesus!" the woman groaned in obvious dismay, shock, and increasing panic. She made a fast bee-line for the door.

He caught her by one arm and pulled her back.

She struggled to be free, more of a handful than he expected, because he found it difficult to hold her and his knife, at one and the same time. It was just lucky for her, though, that he wasn't

keen to kill her immediately, or she would have been almost as easily dispatched as her dog.

He dropped the knife, freeing that hand to use on her, too. Seeing the knife drop, she dropped to have at it. Ken, though, had anticipated just that and went down with her, confident that he knew more about martial-arts than some tart who paddled the asses of subservient perverts who stripped naked, lined up, and passively bent over, for her benefit.

She, though, made up for her lack of expertise by utilizing her intuitive sense of what was needed for her continued survival. If her fighting zeal soon began to fail her, it only did so when it somehow dawned on her, even through her fear, that he wasn't taking advantage nearly as quickly as he could have, possibly because of the undeniable eroticism of their rolling around on the floor.

Many of her customers had their little quirks, their little games. If Ken's needs and quirks were a little more complex than most, that didn't mean that they weren't ritual foreplay just the same.

That she was capable of such reasoning pathetically pinpointed how much she recognized Ken's advantage, emphasized by her dead dog not three feet from them.

Since he had certainly never had any intentions of taking advantage of this woman's fantasies, Ken was more than a little surprised when she was suddenly so eager to unfasten his trousers to give his hard cock ready access to the warmth of her pussy.

She grunted loudly as he obliged and stuck his hardness fast and deep inside her. For the moment, she was caught within ecstasy more powerful than anything she'd ever experienced during more ordinary game play for which her regular clientele paid her. There was no way she could equate this with anything that had ever happened to her before. It was unique, its edge honed by aspects of seemingly real danger.

If she was surprised by the resulting cataclysmic pleasure that left her limp and drained in its aftermath, Ken's surprise

was in realizing he was no longer as much the master of himself as he'd once imagined.

"That was good, honey," she said when it was over and done, feeling safer in the calm after the storm. "That was, in fact, very, very, very good."

"But it didn't make me any less anxious to hear all you have to tell me about Johan Darnel, Miss Tenkaarn," he said, her body still pinned securely beneath him. He rose slightly on his arms for a better view of her sweaty and flushed face.

"Is that who you think I am, stud-man?" she asked. "Heidi Tenkaarn?"

"And, I suppose you're *not?*" Just the way he said it indicated how he thought otherwise.

"You stick with me, and keep on sticking me like you just did, honey, and forget Heidi," she said, raising her right hand to move his tousled blond hair off his damp forehead. "I can show you a good time, can't I? Didn't I just prove it? Heidi, on the other hand, has given up the business. She's out of it for good."

"*Out,* meaning dead?" he asked.

"Dead?" she responded with a smile. She felt more confident, safer. Granted, this handsome sonofabitch had her going there for awhile, but she had finally figured him out. Oh, his type of fun and games was a little more exotic and rough than she was used to (God knew, the dog killing was almost too kinky, but she could handle even that). The money he paid her certainly, at least this time, was enough to cover the trauma she'd been put through. "No, stud, Heidi isn't dead. But, as I said, she's no longer in the business."

"Why don't you tell me just what kind of business she's in, then?" Ken suggested. He didn't know what kind of bullshit this broad was trying to pile on him, but he was willing, at least for the moment, to see what she could come up with in her effort to keep hidden whatever it was she knew about Johan Darnel's whereabouts that Ken was determined to have from her.

CHAPTER SEVENTEEN

KEN COULD SEE HOW the mistake was made. If the woman who emerged from the backroom of the small flower shop to ask if she could help him was a little older than Marie Sprakgarden, who had replaced her at 5 Kalorstraat, she had the same coloring and was approximately the same height. Ken tried to imagine her out of her simple apron and smock, done up in costume, complete with trailing bullwhip or cat-'o-nine-tails.

"I'm looking for this man." Ken extended the photograph of Johan Darnel. "I'm rather hoping you might tell me where he is."

The minute she looked at the picture, he could tell he'd finally struck pay dirt. Heidi Tenkaarn knew Darnel all right. Now, if Ken could only take it from there! He was tired of coming up against blank walls. He'd turned up zero in Egypt, looking for Troy Candle; zilch in Rome, looking for Denver Rheingold. If Heidi didn't give some signs of directing him to Darnel, he wasn't quite sure where he'd turn next.

For a moment, he thought she was going to begin denials. This would have been a royal pain in the ass. If she knew something, she would end up telling him; he just wished he could convince her of that before they were both caused a lot of unnecessary delay, time, and effort.

She didn't deny anything, though. She merely handed back the photograph, and said, "Yes, I know him. What are you, then, a cop?"

"You have any idea why the police might be looking for

him?" Ken asked, denying nothing; admitting nothing.

She shrugged shoulders made muscular by how often, in her other life, she'd wielded a disciplinary whip or paddle.

"Why don't you let me put the 'closed' sign on the door?" she said, moving passed him. Just the way she walked, told him that she wasn't preparing to make any break for freedom. "I doubt it would be good business to have a customer walk in and find me being given the third-degree by a plainclothesman."

She reached the door, turned over the sign already attached to the glass with a string and suction cup, and, then, she pulled the blind to give them even more privacy.

"Actually, I don't know beans about Johan," Heidi said, moving back into the room. She leaned against the counter and reached unthreateningly into her apron pocket for a cigarette and lighter. She lit the former with the latter, not bothering to offer Ken one; she took an exceptionally deep drag, and, then, blew smoke. "This led me to suspect he was a cop, or someone the cops were after. While none of my clientele was ever very talkative, they usually let something slip, somewhere along the line, about what they did, who they were. Not Johan. You say his last name is Darnel? She took another inhale of smoke in emphasis. "All that time, I didn't even know his last name."

"When did you last see him?" Ken asked. She was being extremely cooperative, but there was a definite edge of nervousness in her and to her voice. Normally, Ken might have attributed it to her still assuming he was police. However, any woman who had been in the profession she had once excelled in should have been used to dealing with cops by now.

She couldn't remember just exactly the last time she'd seen Johan. Anyway, that's what she said. She obliged by providing an estimated date which was near enough for Ken to confirm she was possibly the last person to see Darnel before his disappearance.

"He's missing," Ken said.

"Oh?" Heidi said and looked surprised; surprise could always be faked. "Did you ever tell me if he was a cop or a criminal?"

"No."

"He has a wife somewhere, does he?" she asked. "Two or three snot-nosed kids, all wondering where daddy has gotten himself off to?"

"Why don't you let me ask the questions?" Ken suggested.

She shrugged, as if she really wasn't all that interested. Ken, though, sensed otherwise. A broad who nightly pulled off her class act with whips and chains, now masquerading successfully as a typical Dutch flower girl, was undoubtedly a very competent actress.

Someone tried the front door, making Ken and Heidi glance nervously toward the sudden sound. Apparently, though, it was just a frustrated customer, because additional attempts at entry soon aborted.

"How long is this interrogation going to last, huh?" Heidi asked. "I don't make so much money selling flowers that I can afford to lock up shop in the middle of the workday."

"I imagine you made a lot more money on the Kalorstraat," Ken said, sitting the edge of a marble table on which sat three massive flower arrangements waiting pick-up or delivery.

"Yes, well, this life has its compensations, I assure you," Heidi said. Her cigarette was down to its butt. She searched for an ashtray on the counter, found it, and stubbed out the very last of her smoke. She looked momentarily as if she were going to light up another, but, then, apparently, changed her mind.

"Would you mind telling me why you decided to change professions?" Ken asked.

"As if you have to wonder," she said, as if the answer to his question was obvious. "I'm not getting any younger, am I? I just didn't still want to be trying to peddle my tired ass when I was eighty."

Certainly, it was a viable explanation, but Ken saw Heidi not yet having reached the point where she needed to throw in the towel. If she wasn't as pretty as she had been, she still had more looks than a lot of those girls beckoning to men from window seats. Not only that, but, having specialized, as

she had, would have kept her in demand long after her looks began more noticeably to fade. Regular customers wouldn't like their regular routines interrupted by switching from the tried and true to the new and who-knew-what. Granted, Heidi had left them with an obviously well-qualified substitute, by way of Marie Sprakgarden, but still….

"I always wanted to sell flowers," Heidi said, possibly having sensed him not really convinced. "I'd saved a little money, so when this place became available, I just decided, 'Why the hell not?'"

"The way I have it figured," he said, scooting to a firmer sitting position on the tabletop, "is that you left the bondage-and-discipline business, and entered the flower business, just about the same time Johan Darnel dropped out of sight."

"Really?" Heidi sounded as if that sequence of events had never really crossed her mind. "You might be right, but I can assure that, if you are right, it's purely coincidental, one having nothing whatsoever to do with the other."

"Would you mind if I conjecture something other than coincidence?" Ken asked. He reached for one of the white carnations in the nearest large flower arrangement, broke off its blossom and a couple inches of its pale green stem, and threaded the latter through the buttonhole of his suit coat.

"You can conjecture all you like," Heidi said, "as long as you recognize it for the conjecture it is."

"Johan Darnel, at the time of his last session with you, was out to find someone who could help him go underground; someone who might even arrange to get him out of town; you certainly handy. Being grateful for your help, he might have handed over a substantial bit of additional money for your services (sexual and otherwise), which allowed you to buy this shop."

"I wish!" Heidi said with an accompanying laugh that had touches of sarcasm as well as genuine amusement.

Ken readjusted the carnation in his lapel and, while at it, the position of his cock along his left thigh.

"I'd be interested in locating Darnel—dead *or* alive," he said,

reached into his pants pocket, and pulled out a wad of Euros which he began counting off. The monetary sum had reached a considerable amount when he stopped, folded the bills over, and extended the whole lot toward the woman.

"Of course," Heidi said but didn't take the money.

Ken put all the cash back into his pocket and eyed her with an expression that said she was stupid to play little games with him, when he'd tried so hard to handle it in a civilized manner with money.

"Let me tell you a little story," he said finally, "that just might possibly jar your memory as regards Darnel."

Obviously, she figured, and rightly, that if he had a story to tell, he would tell it, no matter her objections. She continued to look ill-at-ease, as well she might. Ken was looking and talking less like a policeman, more like man who knew what he wanted, was able to spot someone who had what he wanted, and would eventually have it, no matter the damages and consequences.

"It has been rumored, recently, within my ear-shot, that there was once a very pretty lady, skilled in certain arenas of sensual amusement like you once were, who, one day, while in a session with a customer had him up and die on her. I suppose nothing like that ever happened to you?"

"Thank God, never!" Heidi said and truly looked as if she wished, more and more, that Ken was the hell out of there.

"How do you think *you* might have reacted to such a scenario?" he asked. Yes, Heidi Tenkaarn was a very good actress, indeed. Ken doubted, though, even she was up to the truly stellar performance his convincing would require.

"I would have called the police, what else?" she said.

"Aren't you saying that just because you think I'm a policeman?" he asked.

"You *are* a policeman, then?" she queried, as if something about the way he asked his question insinuated she might have always been mistaken in thinking him so.

"What do you suppose the police would have said if suddenly called in on that particular scene?" he asked, ignoring Heidi's

query. "Here's a male corpse with chafe marks on its wrists and ankles, whip marks on its back and buttocks. Naked. Dead of what? Of natural causes? Simple heart attack, helped along by one whip lash too many, or one whip lash too hard?"

"Why ask me?" she asked and pushed away from the counter to begin pacing the floor. "I don't get the connection."

"You're sure you don't get the connection?"

"I'm sure," she insisted.

"I have it figured that any such woman in question might well have been scared out of her wits. It must have been pretty traumatic for her, having a body on her hands, having to get rid of it and all. Maybe it was so traumatic that she wanted to make damned sure nothing like it ever happened again. Yes? So, like, maybe, she opened another business. Like, maybe, she opened a flower shop."

"Look, I don't know what Marie told you, but it's hot air!" Heidi said, knowing no one proved anything without a body. All that Marie knew, if she knew anything, was rumor. Heidi couldn't stop rumors, but she had prevented much substance from sticking to them.

"I'm not the police, Heidi," Ken said, confirming what she had come to suspect.

"Who are you, then, exactly, please?" she asked. Not that she was really sure she wanted to know. Hell, maybe he was related to Johan; a brother, maybe.

"All you need to know is that I want to find Johan Darnel," Ken said. "I would prefer finding him alive, but I'll settle for him dead. I will not only be exceedingly generous to whomever gives me information leading to the man or his body, but I will be the epitome of discretion. Discretion, of course, a two-way street, in that I'm sure if the police would be curious to know why one person hid a body, they would be just as curious, if not more so, as to why someone else would have paid so much to have had the body dug up."

"Let me tell you, one final time," Heidi said, "that I know absolutely nothing about Johan Darnel except what I've already

told you. I've not the faintest idea where he or…." She shivered noticeably. "…his body might be."

Her tone was one of dismissal. Dismissal of the subject. Dismissal of Ken. She hoped he would take his cue and leave, but he showed no signs of being so obliging.

Goddamn Johan Darnel! How in the hell had he become the cause of so much trouble in Heidi's life? Oh, she thought, plenty of times, how it would someday be if one of her customers dropped dead during a session. She had especially harbored such thoughts whenever some grey-haired man knocked on her window, or door, begging her to whack his bare flabby ass a good one with a paddle. But Johan Darnel? Jesus, he'd seemed the epitome of good health, and that made it harder to believe that…

"I think you and I know that you know far more than you seem willing to share with me," Ken said, interrupting her train of thought. She welcomed the interruption. It was a horror she had no real desire to relive, even in thoughts.

"Look, Mister!" she said. She had dealt with enough men to know a forceful tone could often cower even the butchest. "You might just as well move your butt on out of here, because I know nothing."

"Maybe; maybe not," Ken said. His widening smile made him look more sinister than amused.

"If you think I'm afraid of you, you are sadly mistaken" she said, getting goose bumps all up and down her arms.

"If you're *not* afraid of me, you very well should be," he said. Something about the calm cadence of his voice made his threat carry far more impact that if he'd spoken in a more malevolent tone.

"Look," Heidi said, afraid, *really* afraid, "if I knew anything, believe me, I would tell you."

She knew things all right. And she was right in that she *would* tell him.

CHAPTER EIGHTEEN

JERRY CROWLSON PICKED UP the Amsterdam Airport Schiphol courtesy phone.

"This is Crowlson," he said, putting his left finger to his left ear to cut some of the noise of fellow passengers who had just cleared Customs and Passport Control with him.

"There's an emergency meeting called, Mr. Crowlson," the voice informed. "Mr. Cheney sent me with the car. Would you please bring your bags directly to the passenger loading area? Ours is the grey Mercedes."

Although Jerry was glad for the convenience of a car and driver, he hoped Powlin Cheney and that man's obnoxious minion, Eldridge Filholden, hadn't decided to start buttering him up at this late date. There was no way their incompetence was left out of his reports regarding this operation. There was no doubt in his mind, whatsoever, that they operated at levels way above their functional, not to mention mental, capabilities. Jesus, if it hadn't been for his CIA information sources, Cheney, Filholden, and he would still be sniffing around Egyptian sand dunes, trying to smell out Ken Mal's farts. If it hadn't been for his CIA contacts, Cheney, Filholden, and he might still be in Paris, trying to find Johan Darnel; Jerry's CIA sources reported Mal left Rome not for Paris but for Amsterdam. If the latter were true, Jerry was pretty sure Darnel had taken a CIA-reported Amsterdam-Paris train to get there.

He spotted the grey Mercedes. He spotted the driver spotting

him; the uniformed chauffeur came quickly to give an assist with the bag.

Jerry couldn't help but wonder what kind of new problem necessitated yet another emergency meeting. He would have thought Cheney and Filholden hadn't been nearly long enough in Amsterdam to have already mucked things up. Then, again, the loose-headed bastards were more likely just pulling another stunt to try and emphasize their supposed importance in all of this. Well, by God, there had better be a genuine cause to warrant Jerry pulled directly from the airport, no time even to freshen up.

"Good trip, sir?" the driver queried, slamming the trunk lid down over Jerry's bag. He was a dark little man with curly black hair, large black eyes, and a nose which looked as if it had a habit of getting in the way of other people's fists.

"Not bad," Jerry admitted and crawled into the plush backseat, having the door slammed shut behind him.

He was glad the car was one of the larger limousines with glass separating him from any chatty driver. He had no great desire to carry on mundane chit-chat about the weather in Amsterdam, compared to the weather in Rome. He'd rather have this time to try and decide, one more time, how he could locate Johan Darnel before Ken Mal and the Russians got him. Some reports hinted Darnel indulged extracurricular activities in Amsterdam's red-light district that were just as interesting as those practiced by Denver Rheingold in the bushes of Rome's Luna Park. In which case, the sooner Jerry found out what those activities were, specifically, the better. Any lead he could get that might aid him in locating Darnel was a lead he wanted ASAP. After all, something convinced Mal to give up on Rheingold in Rome and concentrate, instead, on Darnel in Amsterdam. Something *must* insinuate to Mal that Darnel disappeared in Amsterdam not in Paris. Mal seemed privy to all sorts of information Jerry didn't have, which didn't make Jerry's life any easier. If only Filholden hadn't ordered Mal murdered, none of this need have played out as it was. The Russians should have

been the ones stumbling around in the dark instead of riding on Mal's coattails all of the way to a missing Grey-Zone agent.

Jerry settled back in his seat, extending his legs full-length and groaning in the pure ecstasy of his stretch. Outside was an expanse of typical Dutch countryside that, like the land on which the airport was built, was reclaimed from a large lake drained dry. Jerry preferred Rome to Amsterdam, and he preferred Washington, D.C., to all foreign capitals put together. What he really coveted, though, what he prayed for nightly, was one day landing a plush office job at CIA Headquarters in the Langley suburb of McLean, Virginia. He was beginning to feel the negative effects, physically and mentally, of fieldwork a helluva lot more than he used to.

He dozed, coming awake to find the car on a country road. He leaned forward and tapped the glass partition which the driver lowered slightly for conversation.

"Is it much farther?" Jerry asked, wishing he could at least have had a moment to shower at his hotel. Rather than refresh him, his catnap left him sweaty, more irritable, and with a headache.

"Destination at three o'clock," the driver said. Jerry's head and the car front wheels turned at one and the same time toward the windmill on the horizon.

Jerry dropped back into his seat; the driver once again raised the dividing glass.

Jerry wondered how long it had taken Cheney and Filholden to locate a goddamned windmill in the middle of nowhere for a meeting place. Contrary to popular conception, there weren't all that many windmills left in The Netherlands. Those still fully operational were even rarer. Most had been made obsolete by the invention of electricity.

This particular windmill had been converted, at some time past, into a house; its mill was no longer capable of doing the work it was built to do. Jerry knew that, because the blades were permanently stopped in an "X" configuration. A conventional "cross" would have indicated a momentarily stopped but opera-

tive mill. There were all sorts of "stop" positions that meant different things, like a death in the family, a wedding, even the Queen's birthday. All of which was trivia he'd picked up while taking a course at Quantico about how windmill blade positions had been used extensively by the Allies, during World War II, to pass messages.

The car stopped at the end of the entrance drive. Jerry opened the car door, without waiting to have it done for him by the driver, and got out.

"You're to go right in," the driver instructed. Although he was out of the car, too, it was apparent he'd been told to stay outside. "You can leave your suitcase in the trunk, since I'll be driving you to your hotel directly after the meeting."

Jerry walked to the front door of the mill and opened it, without knocking. He stepped into a living room built to follow the contours of the mill's circumference. The curving wall, directly ahead, was obviously built to conceal the guts of the old mill, and it provided further donut-like definition to the room's layout. Much was immediately lost to sight, around the curve to the left, and the one to the right; no sign of nincompoops Cheney and Filholden.

"Jesus!" Jerry mumbled, wondering what the two idiots were up to now.

He began a slow walk that eventually, frustratingly, came full circle. He was about to open the front door to ask the driver what in the hell was going on when he heard two distinct clicks. One was a door opening. The other was a revolver's hammer being cocked into firing position. Slowly, he turned, without being told to do so.

"Welcome to The Netherlands," Ken Mal said. "Long time no see. And when was the last time we saw each other, Jerry? In London, wasn't it? Just before I left for Egypt. You gave me a farewell present when I left, didn't you? The name of a contact in Egypt who I could 'trust with my life' and who would supply me with all I needed. You did know, by the way, that Glenn Jargreave, your man in question, was most anxious to fix me up

with even more than I asked for."

"Hello, Ken," Jerry said. He couldn't think of much else to say. "I hope you're impressed by the ease with which I walked into this little welcome of yours. Obviously, I've grown careless in my old age."

"And we know what happens to the careless in our line of business, don't we, Jerry?" Ken said. "Why don't you sit down so we can talk a bit? And please—please—do yourself a big favor by not trying anything funny. There's really nothing I would like better, you know, than pulling this trigger, right here and now."

"Then, why don't you?" Jerry asked, surprised by his own calmness. Oh, he wasn't fooling himself into believing that he wasn't neck deep in shit, but something inside of him refused to believe his minutes on Earth were actually all that much less numbered than they had been when he'd first stepped through the front door.

Ken sat in a chair directly across from the one Jerry selected, and said, "I am admittedly rather curious to hear your side of my narrow escape in Tomb 42, Aswan."

"It was all taken out of my hands," Jerry said. "I advised against it, believe me."

"Apparently, you didn't advise hard or loud enough," Ken said. There was a glint of steel in his blue eyes. For the first time that Jerry could ever remember, he thought Ken looked his full thirty-six years. All façade of innocence was gone. What faced Jerry on the other end of that gun was a well-programmed machine that had survived one helluva lot, including an assassination attempt in Tomb 42, Aswan.

"We're all pawns on the chessboard," Jerry said with resignation.

"*You*, certainly, are," Ken said with a cold smile. "But, *I* don't seem to be moving where some of the other players want me to go, do I?"

"You've teamed with the Russians, have you?" Jerry asked. He figured to gather whatever information he could.

"Figured that out by yourself, did you?" Ken asked. "Or, are your CIA spies better informed, these days, than I've come to believe?"

"You're not going to be any safer with the Russians than with us," Jerry warned. "If you find Johan Darnel, the Russians won't risk leaving you around to tell the tale of you having found him for them."

"What do you mean, *if* I find Darnel?" Ken asked.

"Jesus, you've found him?" Jerry responded on cue and wondered if it could be true.

"Would you like to meet him?" Ken asked. "Or, have you met him at sometime in the past? Admittedly, he's a changed man as of late."

"You've *actually* found him?"

Ken stood, the movement of his drawn revolver motioning for Jerry to stand, too. Jerry obeyed.

"He's a little under the weather," Ken said, still smiling without humor, "but, I do want to fulfill my obligation to you, in that it was you, wasn't it, who brought me in to find him?"

"Ken, if you really have him, you should really think seriously before turning him over to the Russians. Our side will pay you big money to get him."

"Your side could now have him, couldn't it?" Ken reminded, "except for your side having decided to kill me before I got the job done."

"The Russians will kill you, make no mistake," Jerry insisted. "Be forewarned. They'll not want you around to tell the world what you stumbled across."

Ken led the way back to the door that had initially concealed him from Jerry, prior to their confrontation. He opened it and motioned Jerry on through.

"Mr. Crowlson, may I present Mr. Darnel?" Ken said, following Jerry into the circular core of the windmill.

A stairway corkscrewed up a shaft the size of the hollow inner sanctum, apparently topping out with another room and floor at a higher level. Where they stood, there was a bed not far

off to one side. On the bed was a body bag; the kind used to ship human remains from a battlefield.

"Not much of poor Mr. Darnel left," Ken said. "He's been sleeping in the damp ground for a little while now, after an apparent unfortunate heart attack, during a rather strenuous bout of S&M fun and games. Hopefully, though, there will be just enough of him left to give the Russians proof-positive of U.S. involvement in the Brimzinsky Incident."

"Implicate the U.S.?" Jerry asked, as if he genuinely couldn't believe his ears. "How in God's name do you figure the Soviets can hope to implicate us in that?"

Ken told him. Not because he doubted, for a moment, that Jerry already knew, but because he wanted Jerry to know just how well-informed Ken had become since Jerry had initially laid on all that bullshit about how the three agents being searched for were important only because of the pipeline they'd afforded the CIA into the Grey Zone.

"Lies!" Jerry said even before Ken came to a finish. "Goddamned lies! You stupid cocksucker; you've let them pull the wool completely over your eyes, haven't you?"

"You'll excuse me if that sounds particularly like sour grapes," Ken said. He motioned Jerry back out of the inner room and into the chair Jerry had previously occupied.

"Listen to me, you silly bastard," Jerry said. He knew how phony it was going to sound, coming at this stage of the game, but he felt he had to make every attempt to keep Ken from turning Darnel's body over to the Russians. "We didn't send those three freelance Grey Zone agents into Russia with any deadly bacteria. It was the Russians who hired them to come in, receive training as couriers, and take out but one of the many toxins developed at Brimzinsky for targeting the free world."

"So, three Grey Zone agents who begin merely as one-time pipelines for the CIA into the Grey Area are, now, suddenly, materialized into agents recruited by the Russians as couriers for Russian-made biological weapons? Give me a break!"

"Loyalties shift, sometimes overnight, especially for those of

you in the Grey Area," Jerry reminded. "Surely, I don't have to remind you of how operatives working for the CIA one day can be working for the Russians the very next day, especially when there are large sums of money involved?"

"You'll excuse me if I somehow find it more conceivable that Candle, Rheingold, and Darnel, were hired by your side to go into Russia with your deadly germ; after which, left running around loose by you until you discovered how the Russians could definitely link them to the U.S. *and* to the contamination at Brimzinsky. You having decided to kill me, too, when you suddenly figured how I just might actually be smart enough to figure out what was behind your search to find them."

"Those three were brought to Brimzinsky by the Russians and given a canister of Russian bacteria, Minnix-TriloniQ," Jerry said, figuring he was losing the battle but still determined to keep up the struggle. "The successful introduction of Minnix-TriloniQ by those men into the U.S. resulted in the first outbreak of Shriners' Disease. You do remember the mystery surrounding the first appearance of that, don't you? Well, now you know why we had so much trouble isolating it. We'd never seen it before, and the Russians weren't about to provide us with any hints as to an antidote."

"You're trying to tell me *that* wouldn't, by now, have long ago been broadcast to the world, if you really had goddamned proof to back it up?"

"We were never able to come up with any concrete proof," Jerry reluctantly admitted, "but we had, and still have, strong suspicions which might still become more concrete if we can ever get a chance to follow up on reports recently smuggled out of Russia about other activities that happened at Brimzinsky. Specifically, a long-occurring leak of the Russian-developed Zilinium-40 that eventually killed everyone and everything there; the leak ongoing when Darnel, Candle, and Rheingold were on-site to pick up the Minnix-TriloniQ; they having survived exposure to it only because they weren't there long

enough to receive fatal doses."

"How long did it take you to come up with that story?" Ken asked. "Surely, not just here and now, spur of the moment."

"It's true, goddamn it!" Jerry insisted. "And even if we can't definitively prove any Russian-Darnel connect by having his body put at our disposal for an autopsy, there might still be enough residual Zilinium-40 present in him for us to devise an antidote or vaccine for it to be used if and when the Russians ever decide to use it on us like they used Minnix-TriloniQ. If you let the Russians have Darnel's body, they'll dispose of it and any immediate chance we might have to link it to the Brimzinsky facility. Certainly, we'll have less chance of ever developing an antidote or vaccine before any sneak-attack in which the Russians chose to use it against us."

"Once again, 'my friend', you could have had Darnel's corpse, and its contents, for whatever research purposes you could have ever wanted, if you'd simply let me proceed with finding it for you!" Ken reminded.

"Can I help it if Eldridge Filholden is a goddamned fool?" Jerry protested vehemently.

"It was Filholden, then, who gave the order for my termination, was it?" Ken asked. Jerry had merely confirmed what Ken's sources had already told him. Not that Filholden's involvement in any way absolved Jerry. Obviously, Jerry hadn't lifted a goddamned finger. And it was more than likely that if the tables were presently turned, he wouldn't hesitate to carry out Ken's termination.

"Filholden thought you might figure out what was happening and make bargains with the enemy," Jerry said.

"Well, he must be frustrated as all hell, knowing that, because of his fuck-up, that's exactly what happened," Ken said.

"Would you please just think out what all of this means to you?" Jerry pressed on. "Just think about it, damn it! The Russians eliminated Troy Candle, and Denver Rheingold. Do you think they're going to just let you…?"

"Just one goddamned minute, here!" Ken interrupted. "You're

just a little confused here, aren't you? What do you mean, the *Russians* eliminated Candle and Rheingold?"

"Sure they did," Jerry said. "Did they tell you differently? Did they tell you *we* did it? Hell, no, we didn't do it. We would have given our left testicles to get either of those two, alive, or dead, into our hands. The Russians beat us to them, muddying up the waters by leaving a few more dead men, like Gregory Ohm, and Giovani Corso, along the way. You can bet that whoever grabbed Denver Rheingold for them, and killed the Corso kid in the bargain, is no more alive today than Ohm is for having successfully taken out Troy Candle for them at Aswan."

"If the Russians were so hot to destroy evidence, do you want to tell me why they left Candle in Tomb 42 to be discovered by some jackass tourist?"

"Candle's body was obviously scheduled for pickup later," Jerry said. "Few people usually bother with Tomb 42. It was just the Russians bad luck that some amateur Belgian Egyptologist bribed his way inside. As it turned out, it didn't much matter, anyway. By the time we found out, the Russians had already moved in, done a bit of grave robbing, and gotten away with Candle's corpse."

Ken saw where there was the possibility that Dilah might have arranged for a replay of the grave-robbing scene, complete with an already empty coffin, to put the blame on the Americans and bring Ken into the Russian camp. Ken had certainly been a plum ripe for the picking, considering the shitty hand the Americans had dealt him. Certainly, Dilah was smart enough to see, what with Ken's connections into the Grey Area, what an asset he might be in locating the last remaining contaminated man, Johan Darnel, for her side.

There was, of course, the question as to why Dilah allowed Ken to go first to Rome in an attempt to locate Rheingold if, as Jerry suggested, Rheingold had already been taken care of by the Russians by then. But even that action (or, rather, that inaction), by Dilah could be explained away, by just supposing she was less likely to tip her hand if she let Ken proceed at his own

speed. Sooner or later, he would have made it to Amsterdam for the last missing piece of the puzzle. What with the progress (or, rather, lack thereof), of the Americans, Dilah could well have felt she was safe to allow Ken the time he needed to reach his own blank wall in Rome. If the Americans ever did show any seemingly sudden spurt toward closing in on Darnel in Amsterdam, Dilah could, then, have moved forward with suggestions that Ken and she move more quickly to The Netherlands.

"Don't be a fool, Ken!" Jerry warned. "There's no way the Russians are going to leave any loose ends to this operation. And you show all indication of being just such a loose end."

"Would you like to propose a solution to the mystery of the dead man you left in my London flat?" Ken asked. "I suppose he wasn't sent by the U.S. special projects unit to do me in, you happening to kill him by accident because you hadn't yet been clued in, yet, on how your CIA operation was interfering where it shouldn't?"

"Jesus!" Jerry said. "The Russians really have managed to tie everything up for you in an apparently neat little ribbon, haven't they?"

"Which doesn't offer any alternative explanation, does it?" Ken reminded.

"How about this one?" Jerry suggested. "The man who was paid to take out Gregory Ohm spots his talking to you, leaving him to think that Ohm might have passed something on to you, inadvertently, or otherwise, that he shouldn't have. He proceeds to terminate Ohm and then, spur of the moment, decides to take care of you, too, just in case something important *was* passed. Later, though, my having killed him before he could kill you, his bosses decide to let you live for a while longer. After all, what did Ohm know about anything to pass on to you anyway? The Russians were careful enough not to identify themselves, or their hidden agenda, when contracting Ohm to take out Candle. Besides, your value in helping them locate the still missing Darnel, if manageable, must have been obviously plain to them, what with your contacts within the Grey Zone; just as it was so

obviously plain to me."

Ken shot him. Not because Jerry's reasoning had come out, in the end, sounding any less plausible than Dilah's spiel. He shot him because Ken refused to be a pawn sacrificed on anybody's game board. The sooner all the players in the shitty game realized that, the better off Ken figured he was going to be.

CHAPTER NINETEEN

DILAH EMPTIED ALL SIX SHOTS into the bed, the revolver giving off muted popping sounds as bullets exited the silencer that screwed securely to the gun barrel.

There was a moment of pregnant silence following the last shot, interrupted by the overly loud click of a table lamp being switched on by Ken who sat in a chair until then concealed by darkness.

Immediately realizing that she had somehow been expected, that Ken had planned for just this moment, in advance, Dilah aimed the gun, still in her hand, and pulled the trigger. Ken didn't even flinch or dodge. He knew the gun was empty. He'd counted the shots, having figured she'd have had sense enough to leave at least one or two bullets as backup. That she hadn't had lowered his estimation of her competence.

"So, it was the Russians, then, all along, huh?" Ken asked, although it wasn't a question. His gun, suddenly in his hand, kept Dilah affixed to the spot. "All of this was one big elaborate mop-op operation to make sure the Americans didn't get evidence to tie the Russians, even tentatively, to any biological experiments at Brimzinsky."

Dilah didn't answer. Ken hardly expected her to. However, that didn't prevent him from continuing his one-sided conversation.

"How, I wonder, did you set up our meeting in Aswan?" he mused. "Quite well-timed, wasn't it? You right there, on the spot when my assassin, drew his knife to stick me in the back.

Coincidence? Or, did you have a double-agent feeding you information from the enemy camp? Is Glenn Jargreave yours as well as the American's?"

After all, it wasn't *only* within the freelance Grey Area arena that agents changed sides, or worked for *two* masters, although such occurrences were definitely more frequent in the former than in the latter.

"Dilah?" Ken pressed. "Was it Jargreave who told you I was being set up for murder by the Americans? Was it Jargreave who gave you the opportunity you'd been waiting for to bring me over to your side with tales of U.S. involvement in the Brimzinsky Incident?"

Dilah still didn't say a thing. In the end, it didn't much matter to Ken who told her what, when. Nor did it really matter to him who was responsible for the deaths at Brimzinsky, or for the deaths from Shiners' Disease, or for the deaths of Troy Candle, Denver Rheingold, Johan Darnel, Gregory Ohm, Giovani Corso, or whoever else might have ended up dead along the way. Long ago, Ken had given up on moral judgments as to whom was right or wrong in the constant bids made for world domination. As far as he was concerned, it was all a matter of so many pots calling so many kettles black.

In the end, it was just important to Ken that Ken looked out for himself, made sure he had plenty of money, a car, a roof over his head, food in his stomach, warm clothes on his back.

Of major importance was that Ken remained alive, no matter how many people died around him.

So, he squeezed off the trigger of the gun in his hand.

CHAPTER TWENTY

ORAN LANGE BROUGHT THE SMALL leather pouch into the room and placed it on the desk.

"Well?" Powlin Cheney asked, leaning back in the large swivel chair whose springs squeaked (he refused to get them oiled, because the sounds had, more than once, kept him from dozing when he shouldn't have). He pyramided his fingers beneath his chin.

"It's a positive I.D., sir," Oran said.

"You're sure?" Powlin asked. There could be no mistake here. He had to be sure the merchandise was genuine.

"It's his, all right," Oran said, nodding toward the pouch on the desk top. "No doubt whatsoever, confirmed by an x-ray taken when Darnel was brought in on a CIA operation two years ago; apparently, he decided to keep it as a memento, or, more likely, as a back-up, when and if ever needed on some compromised assignment elsewhere."

"Very well, then, thank-you," Powlin said by way of dismissal.

Oran did a smart about-face, betraying his recent exit from the military into the intelligence network, and left the office. He closed the door behind him.

Powlin sat for a few moments in complete silence and then came forward amid more squeaking of his chair. He reached for the leather pouch, shifting it and its content from hand to hand before finally relaxing the tightly pulled drawstring. He upended the bag and dropped what was inside, with a clatter, to his desktop.

Johan Darnel's false tooth, inserted in his mouth prior to his participation, as a freelancer, in a previous CIA operation, to conceal cyanide for the easiest way out of any take-no-prisoners situation, was seeming proof that Ken Mal did, indeed, have what he said he had—Darnel's body. Obviously, a dead Johan Darnel, unless Mal had sadistically extracted the tooth from a man still alive. Somehow, Mal had managed to do what all of the American agents, CIA and otherwise, plus all of the Russian agents, had been unable to do.

And Mal was offering the Americans the prize which existed at the end of how many dead men, including—most likely— the now-missing Jerry Crowlson. The only reason Mal was ready to deal, now, was only likely because he had finally realized what Powlin knew all along: the Soviets, to cover their collective ass, would see Ken Mal dead the minute he turned over Darnel's body to them. Mal was simply too smart not to figure out why the dead man's body was so important to both sides.

Not that Mal was prepared to do any big favor for the Americans, just because he'd detected chicanery on the Soviet side. If the Russians had had all intentions of terminating Mal, the Americans had made their own attempt and failed. Mal had outwitted them all, coming out on top, in the end, and certainly in an excellent position to bargain.

Apparently, Mal had decided to deal with the Americans, feeling he could get from them the best price for the package being offered. Oh, the Russians would have been able to match the asking price, even add to it. For that matter, the Red Chinese might have, likewise, matched or enlarged it; whatever lethal bugs the Soviets were testing to use on the U.S. just might (considering presently strained Sino-Soviet relations), be used even sooner on Russia's Oriental neighbors.

It wasn't just money, though, for which Mal was asking. What "something else" he wanted was something the Americans, of all potential buyers of Darnel's corpse, could most easily provide. Not that the Russians, Chinese, or whomever else, wouldn't likely have managed it, too, if given the chance, and

the time, especially upon realizing how important Mal considered it as part of any deal.

Mal had been brought in by Jerry Crowlson to find one or more of the three missing agents for the U.S., hadn't he? He had found one of them, hadn't he? If Eldridge Filholden hadn't ordered Mal's termination, there was at least the possibility that Mal would have turned Darnel' body over to the Americans once he'd found it. Turned it over, too, for an asking price a little less exorbitant than the one he was now asking.

Filholden was a fool! Powlin had realized that for a long time. Crowlson had realized that pretty much from the get-go.

Filholden had independently given the order to terminate Mal, and Crowlson's big mistake had been in not making any move to countermand that order. In fact, Crowlson actually proceeded to take whatever steps were necessary to carry out Filholden's directive. As a result, Crowlson was probably now dead. As for Filholden...?

Powlin felt the chill run the length of his spine. He couldn't help but wonder if Mal realized that Powlin really had had nothing whatsoever to do *directly* with the order Filholden had given, quite on his own initiative (agents who wanted on the fast track were often expected to use their own initiative) to terminate Mal. If Powlin hadn't countered the order, it was because he had left things in charge of Filholden, falsely having assumed that the man had known what in the hell he was doing. Powlin had other irons in the fire besides this operation, so it was necessary for him, continually, to delegate authority. If, in the end, it could be reasoned that Powlin was guilty, because he was Filholden's superior, then that reasoning could likewise be carried even further. Powlin had superiors who had superiors, all of whom could be rationalized to share some of the blame by mere association. Surely, Mal's need for revenge wouldn't be stretched to such extremes!

Was Powlin afraid of Mal? Able to bear witness to the manner and means by which Mal would and did go to eliminate those he considered guilty of crimes against him, was Powlin actually

afraid he, too, was being set up by Mal for eventual termination, although it had been Filholden, and not Powlin, who had set the Mal kill plan into operation? Surely, Mal had the capacity to make certain distinctions without overworking his point.

Powlin picked up the telephone, knowing that Mal might still pull a fast one by taking the money and delivering a substitute body, if he delivered a body at all. Just because Mal had obliged Powlin with a fake tooth identifiable as having come from Johan Darnel's mouth didn't mean he would come through with the Russian-incriminating Zilinium-40-contaminated body. On the other hand, Mal had to have some kind of code of conduct, didn't he? So far, he had seen himself always in the right, always someone else finking out on a deal. Surely if Mal promised a delivery, he would meet it, if just to prove the point that he had always been prepared to deal honorably if he'd only been given the chance to do so.

When Powlin finally got around to hanging up the telephone, he had made three calls, and, in the process, had fully committed himself and the American government to the acquisition of Johan Darnel's corpse from Ken Mal.

"He will be much pleased to hear that," the voice had said at the other end of Powlin's last call. Not Mal's voice. Mal was far too clever to have sat waiting at the other end of the telephone number he'd supplied for contact purposes. Telephone numbers could be traced, even as that one had been traced, to a flea-ridden hotel room across town. Arresting the man found there would have accomplished nothing except interrupted communication. That man was merely a middle-clog nonentity with few—if any—clues or answers.

Eldridge Filholden and the money arrived in Powlin's office at one and the same time, although the latter was carried in by Mark Zanden, assigned to the financial sector of the special projects group. Powlin checked the bag and signed for it and its contents. When Zanden left, Powlin turned his full attention on Filholden.

"At exactly four-fifteen, a grey Mercedes will pull up out front," Powlin said. "You are to take this suitcase into the car with you, and, thereafter, follow whatever instructions are given you by the driver to get you to a delivery point that will be verbally identified for you by your driver as, 'Queen captures pawn.' Do you understand?"

Eldridge certainly understood all that he *had a need to* understand. If Powlin would have wanted him to know any more, he would have told him.

He took the suitcase, vaguely wondering what it was payment for. That Filholden was presently involved in the search for the three missing Grey Zone agents might, or might not, have had something to do with it. As it seemed little more than a simple delivery, however, it might merely have concerned a case altogether different, Filholden having been chosen simply because he was convenient, at the moment, to act as courier.

At four-fifteen, exactly, the grey Mercedes pulled up to the curb out front, and, suitcase in hand, Eldridge Filholden, got into the car.

At six o'clock, Powlin received a phone call notifying him that the men and electronics assigned to track the car had all lost all contact with it.

"Goddamned fucking incompetents!" Powlin bellowed, slamming down the receiver; it was all an act. Mal would have known the car was being monitored, and Powlin had known all along that Mal would know. Mal would have taken precautions, and Powlin had known that, too. Mal, as Powlin had painfully learned throughout this whole episode, was nobody's fool.

When the body bag containing the remains of Johan Darnel was delivered to Powlin's office the next morning at two o'clock, Eldridge Filholden was already two hours dead.

ABOUT THE AUTHOR

WILLIAM MALTESE, the internationally bestselling author of novels, short story collections, and his popular Stud Draqual Mystery Series, has published (under various pseudonyms) close to two hundred books in genres including gay and straight erotica, sci-fi, science-fantasy, mystery, romance, western, adventure, espionage, cooking, wine, and children. With a Business/Advertising degree, Maltese enlisted in the U.S. Army, where he achieved and was honorably discharged at a Sergeant (E-5) rank. Presently, he divides his time between the Pacific Northwest and New York City. You can visit his websites or email him at:

www.williammaltese.com
www.myspace.com/williammaltese
www.facebook.com/williammaltese

email: williammaltese@yahoo.com